Memoirs of Mr. Charles J. Yellowplush by William Makepeace Thackeray

The great author of Vanity Fair and The Luck Of Barry Lyndon was born in India in 1811.

At age 5 his father died and his mother sent him back to England. His education was of the best but he himself seemed unable to apply his talents to a rigorous work ethic.

However, once he harnessed his talents the works flowed in novels, articles, short stories, sketches and lectures.

Sadly, his personal life was rather more difficult. After a few years of marriage his wife began to suffer from depression and over the years became detached from reality. Thackeray himself suffered from ill health later in his life and the one pursuit that kept him moving forward was that of writing. In his life time, he was placed second only to Dickens. High praise indeed.

Index of Contents

CHAPTER I

I was born in the year one, of the present or Christian hera, and am, in consquints, seven-and-thirty years old. My mamma called me Charles James Harrington Fitzroy Yellowplush, in compliment to several noble families, and to a sellybrated coachmin whom she knew, who wore a yellow livry, and drove the Lord Mayor of London.

Why she gev me this genlmn's name is a diffiklty, or rayther the name of a part of his dress; however, it's stuck to me through life, in which I was, as it were, a footman by buth.

Praps he was my father—though on this subjict I can't speak suttinly, for my ma wrapped up my buth in a mistry. I may be illygitmit, I may have been changed at nuss; but I've always had genlmnly tastes through life, and have no doubt that I come of a genlmnly origum.

The less I say about my parint the better, for the dear old creatur was very good to me, and, I fear, had very little other goodness in her. Why, I can't say; but I always passed as her nevyou. We led a strange life; sometimes ma was dressed in sattn and rooge, and sometimes in rags and dutt; sometimes I got kisses, and sometimes kix; sometimes gin, and sometimes shampang; law bless us! how she used to swear at me, and cuddle me; there we were, quarrelling and making up, sober and tipsy, starving and guttling by turns, just as ma got money or spent it. But let me draw a vail over the seen, and speak of her no more—its 'sfishant for the public to know, that her name was Miss Montmorency, and we lived in the New Cut.

My poor mother died one morning, Hev'n bless her! and I was left alone in this wide wicked wuld, without so much money as would buy me a penny roal for my brexfast. But there was some amongst our naybors (and let me tell you there's more kindness among them poor disrepettable creaturs, than in half a dozen lords or barrynets) who took pity upon poor Sal's orfin (for they bust out laffin when I called her Miss Montmorency), and gev me bred and shelter. I'm afraid, in spite of their kindness, that my MORRILS wouldn't have improved if I'd stayed long among 'em. But a benny-violent genlmn saw me, and put me to school. The academy which I went to was called the Free School of Saint Bartholomew's the Less—the young genlmn wore green baize coats, yellow leather whatsisnames, a tin plate on the left arm, and a cap about the size of a muffing. I stayed there sicks years; from sicks, that is to say, till my twelfth year, during three years of witch I distinguished myself not a little in the musicle way, for I bloo the bellus of the church horgin, and very fine tunes we played too.

Well, it's not worth recounting my jewvenile follies (what trix we used to play the applewoman! and how we put snuff in the old clark's Prayer-book—my eye!); but one day, a genlmn entered the school-room—it was on the very day when I went to subtraxion—and asked the master for a young lad for a servant. They pitched upon me glad enough; and nex day found me sleeping in the sculry, close under the sink, at Mr. Bago's country-house at Pentonville.

Bago kep a shop in Smithfield market, and drov a taring good trade in the hoil and Italian way. I've heard him say, that he cleared no less than fifty pounds every year by letting his front room at hanging time. His winders looked right opsit Newgit, and many and many dozen chaps has he seen hanging there. Laws was laws in the year ten, and they screwed chaps' nex for nex to nothink. But my bisniss was at his country-house, where I made my first ontray into fashnabl life. I was knife, errint, and stable-boy then, and an't ashamed to own it; for my merrits have raised me to what I am—two livries, forty pound a year, malt-licker, washin, silk-stocking, and wax candles—not countin wails, which is somethink pretty considerable at OUR house, I can tell you.

I didn't stay long here, for a suckmstance happened which got me a very different situation. A handsome young genlmn, who kep a tilbry and a ridin horse at livry, wanted a tiger. I bid at once for the place; and, being a neat tidy-looking lad, he took me. Bago gave me a character, and he my first livry; proud enough I was of it, as you may fancy.

My new master had some business in the city, for he went in every morning at ten, got out of his tilbry at the Citty Road, and had it waiting for him at six; when, if it was summer, he spanked round into the Park, and drove one of the neatest turnouts there. Wery proud I was in a gold-laced hat, a drab coat and a red weskit, to sit by his side, when he drove. I already began to ogle the gals in the carridges, and to feel that longing for fashionabl life which I've had ever since. When he was at the oppera, or the play, down I went to skittles, or to White Condick Gardens; and Mr. Frederic Altamont's young man was somebody, I warrant: to be sure there is very few man-servants at Pentonwille, the poppylation being mostly gals of all work; and so, though only fourteen, I was as much a man down there, as if I had been as old as Jerusalem.

But the most singular thing was, that my master, who was such a gay chap, should live in such a hole. He had only a ground-floor in John Street—a parlor and a bedroom. I slep over the way, and only came in with his boots and brexfast of a morning.

The house he lodged in belonged to Mr. and Mrs. Shum. They were a poor but proliffic couple, who had rented the place for many years; and they and their family were squeezed in it pretty tight, I can tell you.

Shum said he had been a hofficer, and so he had. He had been a sub-deputy assistant vice-commissary, or some such think; and, as I heerd afterwards, had been obliged to leave on account of his NERVOUSNESS. He was such a coward, the fact is, that he was considered dangerous to the harmy, and sent home.

He had married a widow Buckmaster, who had been a Miss Slamcoe. She was a Bristol gal; and her father being a bankrup in the tallow-chandlering way, left, in course, a pretty little sum of money. A thousand pound was settled on her; and she was as high and mighty as if it had been a millium.

Buckmaster died, leaving nothink; nothink except four ugly daughters by Miss Slamcoe: and her forty pound a year was rayther a narrow income for one of her appytite and pretensions. In an unlucky hour for Shum she met him. He was a widower with a little daughter of three years old, a little house at Pentonwille, and a little income about as big as her own. I believe she bullyd the poor creature into marridge; and it was agreed that he should let his ground-floor at John Street, and so add somethink to their means.

They married; and the widow Buckmaster was the gray mare, I can tell you. She was always talking and blustering about her famly, the celebrity of the Buckmasters, and the antickety of the Slamcoes. They had a six-roomed house (not counting kitching and sculry), and now twelve daughters in all; whizz.—4 Miss Buckmasters: Miss Betsy, Miss Dosy, Miss Biddy, and Miss Winny; 1 Miss Shum, Mary by name, Shum's daughter, and seven others, who shall be nameless. Mrs. Shum was a fat, red-haired woman, at least a foot taller than S.; who was but a yard and a half high, pale-faced, red-nosed, knock-kneed, bald-headed, his nose and shut-frill all brown with snuff.

Before the house was a little garden, where the washin of the famly was all ways hanging. There was so many of 'em that it was obliged to be done by relays. There was six rails and a stocking on each, and four small goosbry bushes, always covered with some bit of linning or other. The hall was a regular puddle: wet dabs of dishclouts flapped in your face; soapy smoking bits of flanning went nigh to choke you; and while you were looking up to prevent hanging yourself with the ropes which were strung across and about, slap came the hedge of a pail against your shins, till one was like to be drove mad with hagony. The great slattnly doddling girls was always on the stairs, poking about with nasty flower-pots, a-cooking something, or sprawling in the window-seats with greasy curl-papers, reading greasy novels. An infernal pianna was jingling from morning till night—two eldest Miss Buckmasters, "Battle of Prag,"—six youngest Miss Shums, "In my Cottage," till I knew every note in the "Battle of Prag," and cussed the day when "In my Cottage" was rote. The younger girls, too, were always bouncing and thumping about the house, with torn pinnyfores, and dogs-eard grammars, and large pieces of bread and treacle. I never see such a house.

As for Mrs. Shum, she was such a fine lady, that she did nothink but lay on the drawing-room sophy, read novels, drink, scold, scream, and go into hystarrix. Little Shum kep reading an old newspaper from weeks' end to weeks' end, when he was not engaged in teaching the children, or goin for the beer, or cleanin the shoes: for they kep no servant. This house in John Street was in short a regular Pandymony.

What could have brought Mr. Frederic Altamont to dwell in such a place? The reason is hobvius: he adoared the fust Miss Shum.

And suttnly he did not show a bad taste; for though the other daughters were as ugly as their hideous ma, Mary Shum was a pretty little pink, modest creatur, with glossy black hair and tender blue eyes, and a neck as white as plaster of Parish. She wore a dismal old black gownd, which had grown too short for her, and too tight; but it only served to show her pretty angles and feet, and bewchus figger. Master, though he had looked rather low for the gal of his art, had certainly looked in the right place. Never was one more pretty or more hamiable. I gav her always the buttered toast left from our brexfust, and a cup of tea or chocklate, as Altamont might fancy: and the poor thing was glad enough of it, I can vouch; for they had precious short commons up stairs, and she the least of all.

For it seemed as if which of the Shum famly should try to snub the poor thing most. There was the four Buckmaster girls always at her. It was, Mary, git the coal-skittle; Mary, run down to the public-house for the beer; Mary, I intend to wear your clean stockens out walking, or your new bonnet to church. Only her poor father was kind to her; and he, poor old muff! his kindness was of no use. Mary bore all the scolding like a hangel, as she was: no, not if she had a pair of wings and a goold trumpet, could she have been a greater hangel.

I never shall forgit one seen that took place. It was when Master was in the city; and so, having nothink earthly to do, I happened to be listening on the stairs. The old scolding was a-going on, and the old tune of that hojus "Battle of Prag." Old Shum made some remark; and Miss Buckmaster cried out, "Law, pa! what a fool you are!" All the gals began laffin, and so did Mrs. Shum; all, that is, excep Mary, who turned as red as flams, and going up to Miss Betsy Buckmaster, give her two such wax on her great red ears as made them tingle again.

Old Mrs. Shum screamed, and ran at her like a Bengal tiger. Her great arms vent veeling about like a vinmill, as she cuffed and thumped poor Mary for taking her pa's part. Mary Shum, who was always a-crying before, didn't shed a tear now. "I will do it again," she said, "if Betsy insults my father." New thumps, new shreex; and the old horridan went on beatin the poor girl till she was quite exosted, and fell down on the sophy, puffin like a poppus.

"For shame, Mary," began old Shum; "for shame, you naughty gal, you! for hurting the feelings of your dear mamma, and beating your kind sister."

"Why, it was because she called you a—"

"If she did, you pert miss," said Shum, looking mighty dignitified, "I could correct her, and not you."

"You correct me, indeed!" said Miss Betsy, turning up her nose, if possible, higher than before; "I should like to see you erect me! Imperence!" and they all began laffin again.

By this time Mrs. S. had recovered from the effex of her exsize, and she began to pour in HER wolly. Fust she called Mary names, then Shum.

"Oh, why," screeched she, "why did I ever leave a genteel famly, where I ad every ellygance and lucksry, to marry a creatur like this? He is unfit to be called a man, he is unworthy to marry a gentlewoman; and as for that hussy, I disown her. Thank heaven she an't a Slamcoe; she is only fit to be a Shum!"

"That's true, mamma," said all the gals; for their mother had taught them this pretty piece of manners, and they despised their father heartily: indeed, I have always remarked that, in famlies where the wife is internally talking about the merits of her branch, the husband is invariably a spooney.

Well, when she was exosted again, down she fell on the sofy, at her old trix—more screeching—more convulshuns: and she wouldn't stop, this time, till Shum had got her half a pint of her old remedy, from the "Blue Lion" over the way. She grew more easy as she finished the gin; but Mary was sent out of the room, and told not to come back agin all day.

"Miss Mary," says I,—for my heart yurned to the poor gal, as she came sobbing and miserable down stairs: "Miss Mary," says I, "if I might make so bold, here's master's room empty, and I know where the cold bif and pickles is." "Oh, Charles!" said she, nodding her head sadly, "I'm too retched to have any happytite." And she flung herself on a chair, and began to cry fit to bust.

At this moment who should come in but my master. I had taken hold of Miss Mary's hand, somehow, and do believe I should have kist it, when, as I said, Haltamont made his appearance. "What's this?" cries he, lookin at me as black as thunder, or as Mr. Phillips as Hickit, in the new tragedy of MacBuff.

"It's only Miss Mary, sir," answered I.

"Get out, sir," says he, as fierce as posbil; and I felt somethink (I think it was the tip of his to) touching me behind, and found myself, nex minit, sprawling among the wet flannings and buckets and things.

The people from up stairs came to see what was the matter, as I was cussin and crying out. "It's only Charles, ma," screamed out Miss Betsy.

"Where's Mary?" says Mrs. Shum, from the sofy.

"She's in Master's room, miss," said I.

"She's in the lodger's room, ma," cries Miss Shum, heckoing me.

"Very good; tell her to stay there till he comes back." And then Miss Shum went bouncing up the stairs again, little knowing of Haltamont's return.

I'd long before observed that my master had an anchoring after Mary Shum; indeed, as I have said, it was purely for her sake that he took and kep his lodgings at Pentonwille. Excep for the sake of love, which is above being mersnary, fourteen shillings a wick was a LITTLE too strong for two such rat-holes as he lived in. I do blieve the family had nothing else but their lodger to live on: they brekfisted off his tea-leaves, they cut away pounds and pounds of meat from his jints (he always dined at home), and his baker's bill was at least enough for six. But that wasn't my business. I saw him grin, sometimes, when I laid down the cold bif of a morning, to see how little was left of yesterday's sirline; but he never said a syllabub: for true love don't mind a pound of meat or so hextra.

At first, he was very kind and attentive to all the gals; Miss Betsy, in partickler, grew mighty fond of him: they sat, for whole evenings, playing cribbitch, he taking his pipe and glas, she her tea and muffing; but as it was improper for her to come alone, she brought one of her sisters, and this was genrally Mary,—for he made a pint of asking her, too,—and one day, when one of the others came instead, he told her, very quitely, that he hadn't invited her; and Miss Buckmaster was too fond of muffings to try this game on again: besides, she was jealous of her three grown sisters, and considered Mary as only a child. Law bless us! how she used to ogle him, and quot bits of pottry, and play "Meet Me by Moonlike," on an old gitter: she reglar flung herself at his head: but he wouldn't have it, bein better ockypied elsewhere.

One night, as genteel as possible, he brought home tickets for "Ashley's," and proposed to take the two young ladies—Miss Betsy and Miss Mary, in course. I recklect he called me aside that afternoon, assuming a solomon and misterus hare, "Charles," said he, "ARE YOU UP TO SNUFF?"

"Why sir," said I, "I'm genrally considered tolerably downy."

"Well," says he, "I'll give you half a suffering if you can manage this bisness for me; I've chose a rainy night on purpus. When the theatre is over, you must be waitin with two umbrellows; give me one, and hold the other over Miss Buckmaster: and, hark ye, sir, TURN TO THE RIGHT when you leave the theater, and say the coach is ordered to stand a little way up the street, in order to get rid of the crowd."

We went (in a fly hired by Mr. A.), and never shall I forgit Cartliche's hacting on that memrable night. Talk of Kimble! talk of Magreedy! Ashley's for my money, with Cartlitch in the principal part. But this is nothink to the porpus. When the play was over, I was at the door with the umbrellos. It was raining cats and dogs, sure enough.

Mr. Altamont came out presently, Miss Mary under his arm, and Miss Betsy following behind, rayther sulky. "This way, sir," cries I, pushin forward; and I threw a great cloak over Miss Betsy, fit to smother

her. Mr. A. and Miss Mary skipped on and was out of sight when Miss Betsy's cloak was settled, you may be sure.

"They're only gone to the fly, miss. It's a little way up the street, away from the crowd of carridges." And off we turned TO THE RIGHT, and no mistake.

After marchin a little through the plash and mud, "Has anybody seen Coxy's fly?" cries I, with the most innocent haxent in the world.

"Cox's fly!" hollows out one chap. "Is it the vaggin you want?" says another. "I see the blackin wan pass," giggles out another gentlmn; and there was such a hinterchange of compliments as you never heerd. I pass them over though, because some of 'em were not wery genteel.

"Law, miss," said I, "what shall I do? My master will never forgive me; and I haven't a single sixpence to pay a coach." Miss Betsy was just going to call one when I said that; but the coachman wouldn't have it at that price, he said, and I knew very well that SHE hadn't four or five shillings to pay for a wehicle. So, in the midst of that tarin rain, at midnight, we had to walk four miles, from Westminster Bridge to Pentonwille; and what was wuss, I DIDN'T HAPPEN TO KNOW THE WAY. A very nice walk it was, and no mistake.

At about half-past two, we got safe to John Street. My master was at the garden gate. Miss Mary flew into Miss Betsy's arms, while master begun cussin and swearing at me for disobeying his orders, and TURNING TO THE RIGHT INSTEAD OF TO THE LEFT! Law bless me! his hacting of hanger was very near as natral and as terrybl as Mr. Cartlich's in the play.

They had waited half an hour, he said, in the fly, in the little street at the left of the theater; they had drove up and down in the greatest fright possible; and at last came home, thinking it was in vain to wait any more. They gave her 'ot rum-and-water and roast oysters for supper, and this consoled her a little.

I hope nobody will cast an imputation on Miss Mary for HER share in this adventer, for she was as honest a gal as ever lived, and I do believe is hignorant to this day of our little strattygim. Besides, all's fair in love; and, as my master could never get to see her alone, on account of her infernal eleven sisters and ma, he took this opportunity of expressin his attachment to her.

If he was in love with her before, you may be sure she paid it him back again now. Ever after the night at Ashley's, they were as tender as two tuttle-doves—which fully accounts for the axdent what happened to me, in being kicked out of the room: and in course I bore no mallis.

I don't know whether Miss Betsy still fancied that my master was in love with her, but she loved muffins and tea, and kem down to his parlor as much as ever.

Now comes the sing'lar part of my history.

CHAPTER II

But who was this genlmn with a fine name—Mr. Frederic Altamont? or what was he? The most mysterus genlmn that ever I knew. Once I said to him on a wery rainy day, "Sir, shall I bring the gig down to your office?" and he gave me one of his black looks and one of his loudest hoaths, and told me to mind my own bizziness, and attend to my orders. Another day,—it was on the day when Miss Mary slapped Miss Betsy's face,—Miss M., who adoared him, as I have said already, kep on asking him what was his buth, parentidg, and ediccation. "Dear Frederic," says she, "why this mistry about yourself and your hactions? why hide from your little Mary"—they were as tender as this, I can tell you—"your buth and your professin?"

I spose Mr. Frederic looked black, for I was ONLY listening, and he said, in a voice hagitated by emotion, "Mary," said he, "if you love me, ask me this no more: let it be sfishnt for you to know that I am a honest man, and that a secret, what it would be misery for you to larn, must hang over all my actions—that is from ten o'clock till six."

They went on chaffin and talking in this melumcolly and mysterus way, and I didn't lose a word of what they said; for them houses in Pentonwille have only walls made of pasteboard, and you hear rayther better outside the room than in. But, though he kep up his secret, he swore to her his affektion this day pint blank. Nothing should prevent him, he said, from leading her to the halter, from makin her his adoarable wife. After this was a slight silence. "Dearest Frederic," mummered out miss, speakin as if she was chokin, "I am yours—yours for ever." And then silence agen, and one or two smax, as if there was kissin going on. Here I thought it best to give a rattle at the door-lock; for, as I live, there was old Mrs. Shum a-walkin down the stairs!

It appears that one of the younger gals, a-looking out of the bed-rum window, had seen my master come in, and coming down to tea half an hour afterwards, said so in a cussary way. Old Mrs. Shum, who was a dragon of vertyou, cam bustling down the stairs, panting and frowning, as fat and as fierce as a old sow at feedin time.

"Where's the lodger, fellow?" says she to me.

I spoke loud enough to be heard down the street—"If you mean, ma'am, my master, Mr. Frederic Altamont, esquire, he's just stept in, and is puttin on clean shoes in his bedroom."

She said nothink in answer, but flumps past me, and opening the parlor-door, sees master looking very queer, and Miss Mary a-drooping down her head like a pale lily.

"Did you come into my famly," says she, "to corrupt my daughters, and to destroy the hinnocence of that infamous gal? Did you come here, sir, as a seducer, or only as a lodger? Speak, sir, speak!"—and she folded her arms quite fierce, and looked like Mrs. Siddums in the Tragic Mews.

"I came here, Mrs. Shum," said he, "because I loved your daughter, or I never would have condescended to live in such a beggarly hole. I have treated her in every respect like a genlmn, and she is as innocent now, ma'm, as she was when she was born. If she'll marry me, I am ready; if she'll leave you, she shall have a home where she shall be neither bullyd nor starved: no hangry frumps of sisters, no cross mother-in-law, only an affeckshnat husband, and all the pure pleasures of Hyming."

Mary flung herself into his arms—"Dear, dear Frederic," says she, "I'll never leave you."

"Miss," says Mrs. Shum, "you ain't a Slamcoe nor yet a Buckmaster, thank God. You may marry this person if your pa thinks proper, and he may insult me—brave me—trample on my feelinx in my own house—and there's no-o-o-obody by to defend me."

I knew what she was going to be at: on came her histarrix agen, and she began screechin and roaring like mad. Down comes of course the eleven gals and old Shum. There was a pretty row. "Look here, sir," says she, "at the conduck of your precious trull of a daughter—alone with this man, kissin and dandlin, and Lawd knows what besides."

"What, he?" cries Miss Betsy—"he in love with Mary. Oh, the wretch, the monster, the deceiver!"—and she falls down too, screeching away as loud as her mamma; for the silly creature fancied still that Altamont had a fondness for her.

"SILENCE THESE WOMEN!" shouts out Altamont, thundering loud. "I love your daughter, Mr. Shum. I will take her without a penny, and can afford to keep her. If you don't give her to me, she'll come of her own will. Is that enough?—may I have her?"

"We'll talk of this matter, sir," says Mr. Shum, looking as high and mighty as an alderman. "Gals, go up stairs with your dear mamma."—And they all trooped up again, and so the skrimmage ended.

You may be sure that old Shum was not very sorry to get a husband for his daughter Mary, for the old creatur loved her better than all the pack which had been brought him or born to him by Mrs. Buckmaster. But, strange to say, when he came to talk of settlements and so forth, not a word would my master answer. He said he made four hundred a year reglar—he wouldn't tell how—but Mary, if she married him, must share all that he had, and ask no questions; only this he would say, as he'd said before, that he was a honest man.

They were married in a few days, and took a very genteel house at Islington; but still my master went away to business, and nobody knew where. Who could he be?

CHAPTER III

If ever a young kipple in the middlin classes began life with a chance of happiness, it was Mr. and Mrs. Frederic Altamont. There house at Cannon Row, Islington, was as comfortable as house could be. Carpited from top to to; pore's rates small; furnitur elygant; and three deomestix: of which I, in course, was one. My life wasn't so easy as in Mr. A.'s bachelor days; but, what then? The three W's is my maxum: plenty of work, plenty of wittles, and plenty of wages. Altamont kep his gig no longer, but went to the city in an omlibuster.

One would have thought, I say, that Mrs. A., with such an effeckshnut husband, might have been as happy as her blessid majisty. Nothing of the sort. For the fust six months it was all very well; but then she grew gloomier and gloomier, though A. did everythink in life to please her.

Old Shum used to come reglarly four times a wick to Cannon Row, where he lunched, and dined, and teed, and supd. The pore little man was a thought too fond of wine and spirits; and many and many's the night that I've had to support him home. And you may be sure that Miss Betsy did not now desert her sister: she was at our place mornink, noon, and night; not much to my mayster's liking, though he was too good-natured to wex his wife in trifles.

But Betsy never had forgotten the recollection of old days, and hated Altamont like the foul feind. She put all kind of bad things into the head of poor innocent missis; who, from being all gayety and cheerfulness, grew to be quite melumcolly and pale, and retchid, just as if she had been the most misrable woman in the world.

In three months more, a baby comes, in course, and with it old Mrs. Shum, who stuck to Mrs.' side as close as a wampire, and made her retchider and retchider. She used to bust into tears when Altamont came home: she used to sigh and wheep over the pore child, and say, "My child, my child, your father is false to me;" or, "your father deceives me;" or "what will you do when your pore mother is no more?" or such like sentimental stuff.

It all came from Mother Shum, and her old trix, as I soon found out. The fact is, when there is a mistry of this kind in the house, its a servant's DUTY to listen; and listen I did, one day when Mrs. was cryin as usual, and fat Mrs. Shum a sittin consolin her, as she called it: though, heaven knows, she only grew wuss and wuss for the consolation.

Well, I listened; Mrs. Shum was a-rockin the baby, and missis cryin as yousual.

"Pore dear innocint," says Mrs. S., heavin a great sigh, "you're the child of a unknown father and a misrable mother."

"Don't speak ill of Frederic, mamma," says missis; "he is all kindness to me."

"All kindness, indeed! yes, he gives you a fine house, and a fine gownd, and a ride in a fly whenever you please; but WHERE DOES ALL HIS MONEY COME FROM? Who is he—what is he? Who knows that he mayn't be a murderer, or a housebreaker, or a utterer of forged notes? How can he make his money honestly, when he won't say where he gets it? Why does he leave you eight hours every blessid day, and won't say where he goes to? Oh, Mary, Mary, you are the most injured of women!"

And with this Mrs. Shum began sobbin; and Miss Betsy began yowling like a cat in a gitter; and pore missis cried, too—tears is so remarkable infeckshus.

"Perhaps, mamma," wimpered out she, "Frederic is a shop-boy, and don't like me to know that he is not a gentleman."

"A shopboy," says Betsy, "he a shopboy! O no, no, no! more likely a wretched willain of a murderer, stabbin and robing all day, and feedin you with the fruits of his ill-gotten games!"

More crying and screechin here took place, in which the baby joined; and made a very pretty consort, I can tell you.

"He can't be a robber," cries missis; "he's too good, too kind, for that: besides, murdering is done at night, and Frederic is always home at eight."

"But he can be a forger," says Betsy, "a wicked, wicked FORGER. Why does he go away every day? to forge notes, to be sure. Why does he go to the city? to be near banks and places, and so do it more at his convenience."

"But he brings home a sum of money every day—about thirty shillings—sometimes fifty: and then he smiles, and says it's a good day's work. This is not like a forger," said pore Mrs. A.

"I have it—I have it!" screams out Mrs. S. "The villain—the sneaking, double-faced Jonas! he's married to somebody else he is, and that's why he leaves you, the base biggymist!"

At this, Mrs. Altamont, struck all of a heap, fainted clean away. A dreadful business it was—hystarrix; then hystarrix, in course, from Mrs. Shum; bells ringin, child squalin, suvvants tearin up and down stairs with hot water! If ever there is a noosance in the world, it's a house where faintain is always goin on. I wouldn't live in one,—no, not to be groom of the chambers, and git two hundred a year.

It was eight o'clock in the evenin when this row took place; and such a row it was, that nobody but me heard master's knock. He came in, and heard the hooping, and screeching, and roaring. He seemed very much frightened at first, and said, "What is it?"

"Mrs. Shum's here," says I, "and Mrs. in astarrix."

Altamont looked as black as thunder, and growled out a word which I don't like to name,—let it suffice that it begins with a D and ends with a NATION; and he tore up stairs like mad.

He bust open the bedroom door; missis lay quite pale and stony on the sofy; the babby was screechin from the craddle; Miss Betsy was sprawlin over missis; and Mrs. Shum half on the bed and half on the ground: all howlin and squeelin, like so many dogs at the moond.

When A. came in, the mother and daughter stopped all of a sudding. There had been one or two tiffs before between them, and they feared him as if he had been a hogre.

"What's this infernal screeching and crying about?" says he. "Oh, Mr. Altamont," cries the old woman, "you know too well; it's about you that this darling child is misrabble!"

"And why about me, pray, madam?"

"Why, sir, dare you ask why? Because you deceive her, sir; because you are a false, cowardly traitor, sir; because YOU HAVE A WIFE ELSEWHERE, SIR!" And the old lady and Miss Betsy began to roar again as loud as ever.

Altamont pawsed for a minnit, and then flung the door wide open; nex he seized Miss Betsy as if his hand were a vice, and he world her out of the room; then up he goes to Mrs. S. "Get up," says he, thundering loud, "you lazy, trolloping, mischsef-making, lying old fool! Get up, and get out of this house. You have been the cuss and bain of my happyniss since you entered it. With your damned lies, and novvle rending, and histerrix, you have perwerted Mary, and made her almost as mad as yourself."

"My child! my child!" shriex out Mrs. Shum, and clings round missis. But Altamont ran between them, and griping the old lady by her arm, dragged her to the door. "Follow your daughter, ma'm," says he, and down she went. "CHAWLS, SEE THOSE LADIES TO THE DOOR," he hollows out, "and never let them pass it again." We walked down together, and off they went: and master locked and double-locked the bedroom door after him, intendin, of course, to have a tator-tator (as they say) with his wife. You may be sure that I followed up stairs again pretty quick, to hear the result of their confidence.

As they say at St. Stevenses, it was rayther a stormy debate. "Mary," says master, "you're no longer the merry greatful gal I knew and loved at Pentonwill: there's some secret a pressin on you—there's no smilin welcom for me now, as there used formly to be! Your mother and sister-in-law have perwerted you, Mary: and that's why I've drove them from this house, which they shall not re-enter in my life."

"O, Frederic! it's YOU is the cause, and not I. Why do you have any mistry from me? Where do you spend your days? Why did you leave me, even on the day of your marridge, for eight hours, and continue to do so every day?"

"Because," says he, "I makes my livelihood by it. I leave you, and don't tell you HOW I make it: for it would make you none the happier to know."

It was in this way the convysation ren on—more tears and questions on my missises part, more sturmness and silence on my master's: it ended for the first time since their marridge, in a reglar quarrel. Wery difrent, I can tell you, from all the hammerous billing and kewing which had proceeded their nupshuls.

Master went out, slamming the door in a fury; as well he might. Says he, "If I can't have a comforable life, I can have a jolly one;" and so he went off to the hed tavern, and came home that evening beesly intawsicated. When high words begin in a family drink generally follows on the genlman's side; and then, fearwell to all conjubial happyniss! These two pipple, so fond and loving, were now sirly, silent, and full of il wil. Master went out earlier, and came home later; missis cried more, and looked even paler than before.

Well, things went on in this uncomfortable way, master still in the mopes, missis tempted by the deamons of jellosy and curosity; until a singlar axident brought to light all the goings on of Mr. Altamont.

It was the tenth of January; I recklect the day, for old Shum gev me half a crownd (the fust and last of his money I ever see, by the way): he was dining along with master, and they were making merry together.

Master said, as he was mixing his fifth tumler of punch and little Shum his twelfth or so—master said, "I see you twice in the City to-day, Mr. Shum."

"Well, that's curous!" says Shum. "I WAS in the City. To-day's the day when the divvydins (God bless 'em) is paid; and me and Mrs. S. went for our half-year's inkem. But we only got out of the coach, crossed the street to the Bank, took our money, and got in agen. How could you see me twice?"

Altamont stuttered and stammered and hemd, and hawd. "O!" says he, "I was passing—passing as you went in and out." And he instantly turned the conversation, and began talking about pollytix, or the weather, or some such stuff.

"Yes, my dear," said my missis, "but how could you see papa TWICE?" Master didn't answer, but talked pollytix more than ever. Still she would continy on. "Where was you, my dear, when you saw pa? What were you doing, my love, to see pa twice?" and so forth. Master looked angrier and angrier, and his wife only pressed him wuss and wuss.

This was, as I said, little Shum's twelfth tumler; and I knew pritty well that he could git very little further; for, as reglar as the thirteenth came, Shum was drunk. The thirteenth did come, and its consquinzes. I was obliged to leed him home to John Street, where I left him in the hangry arms of Mrs. Shum.

"How the d—," sayd he all the way, "how the d-dd—the deddy—deddy—devil—could he have seen me TWICE?"

CHAPTER IV

It was a sad slip on Altamont's part, for no sooner did he go out the next morning than missis went out too. She tor down the street, and never stopped till she came to her pa's house at Pentonwill. She was clositid for an hour with her ma, and when she left her she drove straight to the City. She walked before the Bank, and behind the Bank, and round the Bank: she came home disperryted, having learned nothink.

And it was now an extraordinary thing that from Shum's house for the next ten days there was nothing but expyditions into the city. Mrs. S., tho her dropsicle legs had never carred her half so fur before, was eternally on the key veve, as the French say. If she didn't go, Miss Betsy did, or misses did: they seemed to have an attrackshun to the Bank, and went there as natral as an omlibus.

At last one day, old Mrs. Shum comes to our house—(she wasn't admitted when master was there, but came still in his absints)—and she wore a hair of tryumph, as she entered. "Mary," says she, "where is the money your husbind brought to you yesterday?" My master used always to give it to missis when he returned.

"The money, ma!" says Mary. "Why here!" And pulling out her puss, she showed a sovrin, a good heap of silver, and an odd-looking little coin.

"THAT'S IT! that's it!" cried Mrs. S. "A Queene Anne's sixpence, isn't it, dear—dated seventeen hundred and three?"

It was so sure enough: a Queen Ans sixpence of that very date.

"Now, my love," says she, "I have found him! Come with me to-morrow, and you shall KNOW ALL!"

And now comes the end of my story.

The ladies nex morning set out for the City, and I walked behind, doing the genteel thing, with a nosegy and a goold stick. We walked down the New Road—we walked down the City Road—we walked to the Bank. We were crossing from that heddyfiz to the other side of Cornhill, when all of a sudden missis shreeked, and fainted spontaceously away.

I rushed forrard, and raised her to my arms: spiling thereby a new weskit and a pair of crimson smalcloes. I rushed forrard. I say, very nearly knocking down the old sweeper who was hobbling away as fast as posibil. We took her to Birch's; we provided her with a hackney-coach and every lucksury, and carried her home to Islington.

That night master never came home. Nor the nex night, nor the nex. On the fourth day an octioneer arrived; he took an infantry of the furnitur, and placed a bill in the window.

At the end of the wick Altamont made his appearance. He was haggard and pale; not so haggard, however, not so pale as his miserable wife.

He looked at her very tendrilly. I may say, it's from him that I coppied MY look to Miss —. He looked at her very tendrilly and held out his arms. She gev a suffycating shreek, and rusht into his umbraces.

"Mary," says he, "you know all now. I have sold my place; I have got three thousand pounds for it, and saved two more. I've sold my house and furnitur, and that brings me another. We'll go abroad and love each other, has formly."

And now you ask me, Who he was? I shudder to relate.—Mr. Haltamont SWEP THE CROSSING FROM THE BANK TO CORNHILL!!

Of cors, I left his servis. I met him, few years after, at Badden-Badden, where he and Mrs. A. were much respectid, and pass for pipple of propaty.

THE AMOURS OF MR. DEUCEACE

DIMOND CUT DIMOND

The name of my nex master was, if posbil, still more ellygant and youfonious than that of my fust. I now found myself boddy servant to the Honrabble Halgernon Percy Deuceace, youngest and fifth son of the Earl of Crabs.

Halgernon was a barrystir—that is, he lived in Pump Cort, Temple: a wulgar naybrood, witch praps my readers don't no. Suffiz to say, it's on the confines of the citty, and the choasen aboad of the lawyers of this metrappolish.

When I say that Mr. Deuceace was a barrystir, I don't mean that he went sesshums or surcoats (as they call 'em), but simply that he kep chambers, lived in Pump Cort, and looked out for a commitionarship, or a revisinship, or any other place that the Wig guvvyment could give him. His father was a Wig pier (as the landriss told me), and had been a Toary pier. The fack is, his lordship was so poar, that he would be anythink or nothink, to get provisions for his sons and an inkum for himself.

I phansy that he aloud Halgernon two hundred a year; and it would have been a very comforable maintenants, only he knever paid him.

Owever, the young genlmn was a genlmn, and no mistake; he got his allowents of nothing a year, and spent it in the most honrabble and fashnabble manner. He kep a kab—he went to Holmax—and Crockfud's—he moved in the most xquizzit suckles and trubbld the law boox very little, I can tell you. Those fashnabble gents have ways of getten money, witch comman pipple doan't understand.

Though he only had a therd floar in Pump Cort, he lived as if he had the welth of Cresas. The tenpun notes floo abowt as common as haypince—clarrit and shampang was at his house as vulgar as gin; and verry glad I was, to be sure, to be a valley to a zion of the nobillaty.

Deuceace had, in his sittin-room, a large pictur on a sheet of paper. The names of his family was wrote on it; it was wrote in the shape of a tree, a-groin out of a man-in-armer's stomick, and the names were on little plates among the bows. The pictur said that the Deuceaces kem into England in the year 1066, along with William Conqueruns. My master called it his podygree. I do bleev it was because he had this pictur, and because he was the HONRABBLE Deuceace, that he mannitched to live as he did. If he had been a common man, you'd have said he was no better than a swinler. It's only rank and buth that can warrant such singularities as my master show'd. For it's no use disgysing it—the Honrabble Halgernon was a GAMBLER. For a man of wulgar family, it's the wust trade that can be—for a man of common feelinx of honesty, this profession is quite imposbil; but for a real thoroughbread genlmn, it's the esiest and most prophetable line he can take.

It may praps appear curious that such a fashnabble man should live in the Temple; but it must be recklected, that it's not only lawyers who live in what's called the Ins of Cort. Many batchylers, who have nothink to do with lor, have here their loginx; and many sham barrysters, who never put on a wig and gownd twise in their lives, kip apartments in the Temple, instead of Bon Street, Pickledilly, or other fashnabble places.

Frinstance, on our stairkis (so these houses are called), there was 8 sets of chamberses, and only 3 lawyers. These was bottom floar, Screwson, Hewson, and Jewson, attorneys; fust floar, Mr. Sergeant Flabber—opsite, Mr. Counslor Bruffy; and secknd pair, Mr. Haggerstony, an Irish counslor, praktising at the Old Baly, and lickwise what they call reporter to the Morning Post nyouspapper. Opsite him was wrote

MR. RICHARD BLEWITT;

and on the thud floar, with my master, lived one Mr. Dawkins.

This young fellow was a new comer into the Temple, and unlucky it was for him too—he'd better have never been born; for it's my firm apinion that the Temple ruined him—that is, with the help of my master and Mr. Dick Blewitt: as you shall hear.

Mr. Dawkins, as I was gave to understand by his young man, had just left the Universary of Oxford, and had a pretty little fortn of his own—six thousand pound, or so—in the stox. He was jest of age, an orfin who had lost his father and mother; and having distinkwished hisself at Collitch, where he gained seffral prices, was come to town to push his fortn, and study the barryster's bisness.

Not bein of a very high fammly hisself—indeed, I've heard say his father was a chismonger, or somethink of that lo sort—Dawkins was glad to find his old Oxford frend, Mr. Blewitt, yonger son to rich Squire Blewitt, of Listershire, and to take rooms so near him.

Now, tho' there was a considdrable intimacy between me and Mr. Blewitt's gentleman, there was scarcely any betwixt our masters,—mine being too much of the aristoxy to associate with one of Mr. Blewitt's sort. Blewitt was what they call a bettin man; he went reglar to Tattlesall's, kep a pony, wore a white hat, a blue berd's-eye handkercher, and a cut-away coat. In his manners he was the very contrary of my master, who was a slim, ellygant man as ever I see—he had very white hands, rayther a sallow face, with sharp dark ise, and small wiskus neatly trimmed and as black as Warren's jet—he spoke very low and soft—he seemed to be watchin the person with whom he was in convysation, and always flatterd everybody. As for Blewitt, he was quite of another sort. He was always swearin, singing, and slappin people on the back, as hearty as posbill. He seemed a merry, careless, honest cretur, whom one would trust with life and soul. So thought Dawkins, at least; who, though a quiet young man, fond of his boox, novvles, Byron's poems, foot-playing, and such like scientafic amusemints, grew hand in glove with honest Dick Blewitt, and soon after with my master, the Honrabble Halgernon. Poor Daw! he thought he was makin good connexions and real frends—he had fallen in with a couple of the most etrocious swinlers that ever lived.

Before Mr. Dawkins's arrival in our house, Mr. Deuceace had barely condysended to speak to Mr. Blewitt; it was only about a month after that suckumstance that my master, all of a suddin, grew very friendly with him. The reason was pretty clear,—Deuceace WANTED HIM. Dawkins had not been an hour in master's company before he knew that he had a pidgin to pluck.

Blewitt knew this too: and bein very fond of pidgin, intended to keep this one entirely to himself. It was amusin to see the Honrabble Halgernon manuvring to get this poor bird out of Blewitt's clause, who thought he had it safe. In fact, he'd brought Dawkins to these chambers for that very porpos, thinking to have him under his eye, and strip him at leisure.

My master very soon found out what was Mr. Blewitt's game. Gamblers know gamblers, if not by instink, at least by reputation; and though Mr. Blewitt moved in a much lower speare than Mr. Deuceace, they knew each other's dealins and caracters puffickly well.

"Charles you scoundrel," says Deuceace to me one day (he always spoak in that kind way), "who is this person that has taken the opsit chambers, and plays the flute so industrusly?"

"It's Mr. Dawkins, a rich young gentleman from Oxford, and a great friend of Mr. Blewittses, sir," says I; "they seem to live in each other's rooms."

Master said nothink, but he GRIN'D—my eye, how he did grin. Not the fowl find himself could snear more satannickly.

I knew what he meant:

Imprimish. A man who plays the floot is a simpleton.

Secknly. Mr. Blewitt is a raskle.

Thirdmo. When a raskle and a simpleton is always together, and when the simpleton is RICH, one knows pretty well what will come of it.

I was but a lad in them days, but I knew what was what, as well as my master; it's not gentlemen only that's up to snough. Law bless us! there was four of us on this stairkes, four as nice young men as you ever see: Mr. Bruffy's young man, Mr. Dawkinses, Mr. Blewitt's, and me—and we knew what our masters was about as well as thay did theirselfs. Frinstance, I can say this for MYSELF, there wasn't a paper in Deuceace's desk or drawer, not a bill, a note, or mimerandum, which I hadn't read as well as he: with Blewitt's it was the same—me and his young man used to read 'em all. There wasn't a bottle of wine that we didn't get a glass out of, nor a pound of sugar that we didn't have some lumps of it. We had keys to all the cubbards—we pipped into all the letters that kem and went—we pored over all the bill-files—we'd the best pickens out of the dinners, the livvers of the fowls, the forcemit balls out of the soup, the egs from the sallit. As for the coals and candles, we left them to the landrisses. You may call this robry—nonsince—it's only our rights—a suvvant's purquizzits is as sacred as the laws of Hengland.

Well, the long and short of it is this. Richard Blewitt, esquire, was sityouated as follows: He'd an incum of three hundred a year from his father. Out of this he had to pay one hundred and ninety for money borrowed by him at collidge, seventy for chambers, seventy more for his hoss, aty for his suvvant on bord wagis, and about three hundred and fifty for a sepparat establishment in the Regency Park; besides this, his pockit-money, say a hunderd, his eatin, drinkin, and wine-marchant's bill, about two hunderd moar. So that you see he laid by a pretty handsome sum at the end of the year.

My master was diffrent; and being a more fashnable man than Mr. B., in course he owed a deal more mony. There was fust:

Account contrary, at Crockford's	L 3711 0 0
Bills of xchange and I. O. U.'s (but he didn't pay these in most cases)	4963 0 0
21 tailors' bills, in all	1306 11 9
3 hossdealers' do	402 0 0
2 coachbuilder	506 0 0
Bills contracted at Cambridtch	2193 6 8
Sundries	987 10 0

	L 14069 8 5

I give this as a curosity—pipple doan't know how in many cases fashnabble life is carried on; and to know even what a real gnlmn OWES is somethink instructif and agreeable.

But to my tail. The very day after my master had made the inquiries concerning Mr. Dawkins, witch I mentioned already, he met Mr. Blewitt on the stairs; and byoutiffle it was to see how this gnlmn, who had before been almost cut by my master, was now received by him. One of the sweetest smiles I ever saw was now vizzable on Mr. Deuceace's countenance. He held out his hand, covered with a white kid glove, and said, in the most frenly tone of vice posbill, "What! Mr. Blewitt? It is an age since we met. What a shame that such near naybors should see each other so seldom!"

Mr. Blewitt, who was standing at his door, in a pe-green dressing-gown, smoakin a segar, and singing a hunting coarus, looked surprised, flattered, and then suspicious.

"Why, yes," says he, "it is, Mr. Deuceace, a long time."

"Not, I think, since we dined at Sir George Hookey's. By-the-by, what an evening that was—hay, Mr. Blewitt? What wine! what capital songs! I recollect your 'May-day in the morning'—cuss me, the best comick song I ever heard. I was speaking to the Duke of Doncaster about it only yesterday. You know the duke, I think?"

Mr. Blewitt said, quite surly, "No, I don't."

"Not know him!" cries master; "why, hang it, Blewitt! he knows YOU; as every sporting man in England does, I should think. Why, man, your good things are in everybody's mouth at Newmarket."

And so master went on chaffin Mr. Blewitt. That genlmn at fust answered him quite short and angry: but, after a little more flummery, he grew as pleased as posbill, took in all Deuceace's flatry, and bleeved all his lies. At last the door shut, and they both went into Mr. Blewitt's chambers together.

Of course I can't say what past there; but in an hour master kem up to his own room as yaller as mustard, and smellin sadly of backo smoke. I never see any genmln more sick than he was; HE'D BEEN SMOAKIN SEAGARS along with Blewitt. I said nothink, in course, tho I'd often heard him xpress his horrow of backo, and knew very well he would as soon swallow pizon as smoke. But he wasn't a chap to do a thing without a reason: if he'd been smoakin, I warrant he had smoked to some porpus.

I didn't hear the convysation betwean 'em; but Mr. Blewitt's man did: it was,—"Well, Mr. Blewitt, what capital seagars! Have you one for a friend to smoak?" (The old fox, it wasn't only the SEAGARS he was a-smoakin!) "Walk in," says Mr. Blewitt; and they began a chaffin together; master very ankshous about the young gintleman who had come to live in our chambers, Mr. Dawkins, and always coming back to that subject,—saying that people on the same stairkis ot to be frenly; how glad he'd be, for his part, to know Mr. Dick Blewitt, and ANY FRIEND OF HIS, and so on. Mr. Dick, howsever, seamed quite aware of the trap laid for him. "I really don't know this Dawkins," says he: "he's a chismonger's son, I hear; and tho I've exchanged visits with him, I doan't intend to continyou the acquaintance,—not wishin to assoshate with that kind of pipple." So they went on, master fishin, and Mr. Blewitt not wishin to take the hook at no price.

"Confound the vulgar thief!" muttard my master, as he was laying on his sophy, after being so very ill; "I've poisoned myself with his infernal tobacco, and he has foiled me. The cursed swindling boor! he thinks he'll ruin this poor Cheese-monger, does he? I'll step in, and WARN him."

I thought I should bust a-laffin, when he talked in this style. I knew very well what his "warning" meant,—lockin the stable-door but stealin the hoss fust.

Next day, his strattygam for becoming acquainted with Mr. Dawkins we exicuted; and very pritty it was.

Besides potry and the flute, Mr. Dawkins, I must tell you, had some other parshallities—wiz., he was very fond of good eatin and drinkin. After doddling over his music and boox all day, this young genlmn used to sally out of evenings, dine sumptiously at a tavern, drinkin all sorts of wine along with his friend Mr. Blewitt. He was a quiet young fellow enough at fust; but it was Mr. B. who (for his own porpuses, no doubt,) had got him into this kind of life. Well, I needn't say that he who eats a fine dinner, and drinks too much overnight, wants a bottle of soda-water, and a gril, praps, in the morning. Such was Mr. Dawkinses case; and reglar almost as twelve o'clock came, the waiter from "Dix Coffy-House" was to be seen on our stairkis, bringing up Mr. D.'s hot breakfast.

No man would have thought there was anythink in such a trifling cirkumstance; master did, though, and pounced upon it like a cock on a barlycorn.

He sent me out to Mr. Morell's in Pickledilly, for wot's called a Strasbug-pie—in French, a "patty defau graw." He takes a card, and nails it on the outside case (patty defaw graws come generally in a round wooden box, like a drumb); and what do you think he writes on it? why, as follos:—"For the Honorable Algernon Percy Deuceace, &c. &c. &c. With Prince Talleyrand's compliments."

Prince Tallyram's complimints, indeed! I laff when I think of it, still, the old surpint! He WAS a surpint, that Deuceace, and no mistake.

Well, by a most extrornary piece of ill-luck, the nex day punctially as Mr. Dawkinses brexfas was coming UP the stairs, Mr. Halgernon Percy Deuceace was going DOWN. He was as gay as a lark, humming an Oppra tune, and twizzting round his head his hevy gold-headed cane. Down he went very fast, and by a most unlucky axdent struck his cane against the waiter's tray, and away went Mr. Dawkinses gril, kayann, kitchup, soda-water and all! I can't think how my master should have choas such an exact time; to be sure, his windo looked upon the court, and he could see every one who came into our door.

As soon as the axdent had took place, master was in such a rage as, to be sure, no man ever was in befor; he swoar at the waiter in the most dreddfle way; he threatened him with his stick, and it was only when he see that the waiter was rayther a bigger man than hisself that he was in the least pazzyfied. He returned to his own chambres; and John, the waiter, went off for more gril to Dixes Coffy-house.

"This is a most unlucky axdent, to be sure, Charles," says master to me, after a few minits paws, during witch he had been and wrote a note, put it into an anvelope, and sealed it with his big seal of arms. "But stay—a thought strikes me—take this note to Mr. Dawkins, and that pye you brought yesterday; and hearkye, you scoundrel, if you say where you got it I will break every bone in your skin!"

These kind of promises were among the few which I knew him to keep: and as I loved boath my skinn and my boans, I carried the noat, and of cors said nothink. Waiting in Mr. Dawkinses chambus for a few minnits, I returned to my master with an anser. I may as well give both of these documence, of which I happen to have taken coppies:

I.

THE HON. A. P. DEUCEACE TO T. S. DAWKINS, ESQ.

"TEMPLE, Tuesday.

"Mr. DEUCEACE presents his compliments to Mr. Dawkins, and begs at the same time to offer his most sincere apologies and regrets for the accident which has just taken place.

"May Mr. Deuceace be allowed to take a neighbor's privilege, and to remedy the evil he has occasioned to the best of his power if Mr. Dawkins will do him the favor to partake of the contents of the accompanying case (from Strasbourg direct, and the gift of a friend, on whose taste as a gourmand Mr. Dawkins may rely), perhaps he will find that it is not a bad substitute for the plat which Mr. Deuceace's awkwardness destroyed.

"It will also, Mr. Deuceace is sure, be no small gratification to the original donor of the 'pate', when he learns that it has fallen into the hands of so celebrated a bon vivant as Mr. Dawkins.

"T. S. DAWKINS, Esq., &c. &c. &c."

II.

FROM T. S. DAWKINS, ESQ., TO THE HON. A. P. DEUCEACE.

"MR. THOMAS SMITH DAWKINS presents his grateful compliments to the Hon. Mr. Deuceace, and accepts with the greatest pleasure Mr. Deuceace's generous proffer.

"It would be one of the HAPPIEST MOMENTS of Mr. Smith Dawkins's life, if the Hon. Mr. Deuceace would EXTEND HIS GENEROSITY still further, and condescend to partake of the repast which his MUNIFICENT POLITENESS has furnished.

"TEMPLE, Tuesday."

Many and many a time, I say, have I grin'd over these letters, which I had wrote from the original by Mr. Bruffy's copyin clark. Deuceace's flam about Prince Tallyram was puffickly successful. I saw young Dawkins blush with delite as he red the note; he toar up for or five sheets before he composed the answer to it, which was as you red abuff, and roat in a hand quite trembling with pleasyer. If you could but have seen the look of triumph in Deuceace's wicked black eyes, when he read the noat! I never see a deamin yet, but I can phansy 1, a holding a writhing soal on his pitchfrock, and smilin like Deuceace. He dressed himself in his very best clothes, and in he went, after sending me over to say that he would except with pleasyour Mr. Dawkins's invite.

The pie was cut up, and a most frenly conversation begun betwixt the two genlmin. Deuceace was quite captivating. He spoke to Mr. Dawkins in the most respeckful and flatrin manner,—agread in every think he said,—prazed his taste, his furniter, his coat, his classick nolledge, and his playin on the floot; you'd have thought, to hear him, that such a polygon of exlens as Dawkins did not breath,—that such a modist, sinsear, honrabble genlmn as Deuceace was to be seen nowhere xcept in Pump Cort. Poor Daw was complitly taken in. My master said he'd introduce him to the Duke of Doncaster, and heaven knows how many nobs more, till Dawkins was quite intawsicated with pleasyour. I know as a fac (and it pretty well shows the young genlmn's carryter), that he went that very day and ordered 2 new coats, on porpos to be introjuiced to the lords in.

But the best joak of all was at last. Singin, swagrin, and swarink—up stares came Mr. Dick Blewitt. He flung opn Mr. Dawkins's door, shouting out, "Daw my old buck, how are you?" when, all of a sudden, he sees Mr. Deuceace: his jor dropt, he turned chocky white, and then burnin red, and looked as if a stror would knock him down. "My dear Mr. Blewitt," says my master, smilin and offring his hand, "how glad I am to see you. Mr. Dawkins and I were just talking about your pony! Pray sit down."

Blewitt did; and now was the question, who should sit the other out; but law bless you! Mr. Blewitt was no match for my master: all the time he was fidgetty, silent, and sulky; on the contry, master was charmin. I never herd such a flo of conversatin, or so many wittacisms as he uttered. At last, completely beat, Mr. Blewitt took his leaf; that instant master followed him; and passin his arm through that of Mr. Dick, led him into our chambers, and began talkin to him in the most affabl and affeckshnat manner.

But Dick was too angry to listen; at last, when master was telling him some long story about the Duke of Doncaster, Blewitt burst out—

"A plague on the Duke of Doncaster! Come, come, Mr. Deuceace, don't you be running your rigs upon me; I ain't the man to be bamboozl'd by long-winded stories about dukes and duchesses. You think I don't know you; every man knows you and your line of country. Yes, you're after young Dawkins there, and think to pluck him; but you shan't,—no, by — you shan't." (The reader must recklect that the oaths which interspussed Mr. B.'s convysation I have left out.) Well, after he'd fired a wolley of 'em, Mr. Deuceace spoke as cool as possbill.

"Hark ye, Blewitt. I know you to be one of the most infernal thieves and scoundrels unhung. If you attempt to hector with me, I will cane you; if you want more, I'll shoot you; if you meddle between me and Dawkins, I will do both. I know your whole life, you miserable swindler and coward. I know you have already won two hundred pounds of this lad, and want all. I will have half, or you never shall have a penny." It's quite true that master knew things; but how was the wonder.

I couldn't see Mr. B.'s face during this dialogue, bein on the wrong side of the door; but there was a considdrable paws after thuse complymints had passed between the two genlmn,—one walkin quickly up and down the room—tother, angry and stupid, sittin down, and stampin with his foot.

"Now listen to this, Mr. Blewitt," continues master at last. "If you're quiet, you shall have half this fellow's money: but venture to win a shilling from him in my absence, or without my consent, and you do it at your peril."

"Well, well, Mr. Deuceace," cries Dick, "it's very hard, and I must say, not fair: the game was of my startin, and you've no right to interfere with my friend."

"Mr. Blewitt, you are a fool! You professed yesterday not to know this man, and I was obliged to find him out for myself. I should like to know by what law of honor I am bound to give him up to you?"

It was charmin to hear this pair of raskles talkin about HONOR. I declare I could have found it in my heart to warn young Dawkins of the precious way in which these chaps were going to serve him. But if THEY didn't know what honor was, I did; and never, never did I tell tails about my masters when in their sarvice—OUT, in cors, the hobligation is no longer binding.

Well, the nex day there was a gran dinner at our chambers. White soop, turbit, and lobstir sos; saddil of Scoch muttn, grous, and M'Arony; wines, shampang, hock, maderia, a bottle of poart, and ever so many of clarrit. The compny presint was three; wiz., the Honrabble A. P. Deuceace, R. Blewitt, and Mr. Dawkins, Exquires. My i, how we genlmn in the kitchin did enjy it. Mr. Blewittes man eat so much grous (when it was brot out of the parlor), that I reely thought he would be sik; Mr. Dawkinses genlmn (who was only abowt 13 years of age) grew so il with M'Arony and plumb-puddn, as to be obleeged to take sefral of Mr. D's. pils, which 1/2 kild him. But this is all promiscuous: I an't talkin of the survants now, but the masters.

Would you bleeve it? After dinner and praps 8 bottles of wine between the 3, the genlm sat down to ecarty. It's a game where only 2 plays, and where, in coarse, when there's only 3, one looks on.

Fust, they playd crown pints, and a pound the bett. At this game they were wonderful equill; and about supper-time (when grilled am, more shampang, devld biskits, and other things, was brot in) the play stood thus: Mr. Dawkins had won 2 pounds; Mr. Blewitt 30 shillings; the Honrabble Mr. Deuceace having lost 3L. l0s. After the devvle and the shampang the play was a little higher. Now it was pound pints, and five pound the bet. I thought, to be sure, after hearing the complymints between Blewitt and master in the morning, that now poor Dawkins's time was come.

Not so: Dawkins won always, Mr. B. betting on his play, and giving him the very best of advice. At the end of the evening (which was abowt five o'clock the nex morning) they stopt. Master was counting up the skore on a card.

"Blewitt," says he, "I've been unlucky. I owe you, let me see—yes, five-and-forty pounds?"

"Five-and-forty," says Blewitt, "and no mistake!"

"I will give you a cheque," says the honrabble genlmn.

"Oh! don't mention it, my dear sir!" But master got a grate sheet of paper, and drew him a check on Messeers. Pump, Algit and Co., his bankers.

"Now," says master, "I've got to settle with you, my dear Mr. Dawkins. If you had backd your luck, I should have owed you a very handsome sum of money. Voyons, thirteen points at a pound—it is easy to calculate;" and drawin out his puss, he clinked over the table 13 goolden suverings, which shon till they made my eyes wink.

So did pore Dawkinses, as he put out his hand, all trembling, and drew them in.

"Let me say," added master, "let me say (and I've had some little experience), that you are the very best ecarte player with whom I ever sat down."

Dawkinses eyes glissened as he put the money up, and said, "Law, Deuceace, you flatter me."

FLATTER him! I should think he did. It was the very think which master ment.

"But mind you, Dawkins," continyoud he, "I must have my revenge; for I'm ruined—positively ruined by your luck."

"Well, well," says Mr. Thomas Smith Dawkins, as pleased as if he had gained a millium, "shall it be to-morrow? Blewitt, what say you?"

Mr. Blewitt agreed, in course. My master, after a little demurring, consented too. "We'll meet," says he, "at your chambers. But mind, my dear fello, not too much wine: I can't stand it at any time, especially when I have to play ecarte with YOU."

Pore Dawkins left our rooms as happy as a prins. "Here, Charles," says he, and flung me a sovring. Pore fellow! pore fellow! I knew what was a-comin!

But the best of it was, that these 13 sovrings which Dawkins won, MASTER HAD BORROWED THEM FROM MR. BLEWITT! I brought 'em, with 7 more, from that young genlmn's chambers that very morning: for, since his interview with master, Blewitt had nothing to refuse him.

Well, shall I continue the tail? If Mr. Dawkins had been the least bit wiser, it would have taken him six months befoar he lost his money; as it was, he was such a confunded ninny, that it took him a very short time to part with it.

Nex day (it was Thursday, and master's acquaintance with Mr. Dawkins had only commenced on Tuesday), Mr. Dawkins, as I said, gev his party,—dinner at 7. Mr. Blewitt and the two Mr. D.'s as befoar. Play begins at 11. This time I knew the bisness was pretty serious, for we suvvants was packed off to bed at 2 o'clock. On Friday, I went to chambers—no master—he kem in for 5 minutes at about 12, made a little toilit, ordered more devvles and soda-water, and back again he went to Mr. Dawkins's.

They had dinner there at 7 again, but nobody seamed to eat, for all the vittles came out to us genlmn: they had in more wine though, and must have drunk at least two dozen in the 36 hours.

At ten o'clock, however, on Friday night, back my master came to his chambers. I saw him as I never saw him before, namly reglar drunk. He staggered about the room, he danced, he hickipd, he swoar, he flung me a heap of silver, and, finely, he sunk down exosted on his bed; I pullin off his boots and close, and making him comfrabble.

When I had removed his garmints, I did what it's the duty of every servant to do—I emtied his pockits, and looked at his pockit-book and all his letters: a number of axdents have been prevented that way.

I found there, among a heap of things, the following pretty dockyment—

I. O. U. L 4700.
THOMAS SMITH DAWKINS.
Friday, 16th January.

There was another bit of paper of the same kind—"I. O. U. four hundred pounds: Richard Blewitt:" but this, in corse, ment nothink.

Nex mornin, at nine, master was up, and as sober as a judg. He drest, and was off to Mr. Dawkins. At ten, he ordered a cab, and the two gentlmn went together.

"Where shall he drive, sir?" says I.

"Oh, tell him to drive to THE BANK."

Pore Dawkins! his eyes red with remors and sleepliss drunkenniss, gave a shudder and a sob, as he sunk back in the wehicle; and they drove on.

That day he sold out every hapny he was worth, xcept five hundred pounds.

Abowt 12 master had returned, and Mr. Dick Blewitt came stridin up the stairs with a sollum and important hair.

"Is your master at home?" says he.

"Yes, sir," says I; and in he walks. I, in coars, with my ear to the keyhole, listning with all my mite.

"Well," says Blewitt, "we maid a pretty good night of it, Mr. Deuceace. Yu've settled, I see, with Dawkins."

"Settled!" says master. "Oh, yes—yes—I've settled with him."

"Four thousand seven hundred, I think?"

"About that—yes."

"That makes my share—let me see—two thousand three hundred and fifty; which I'll thank you to fork out."

"Upon my word—why—Mr. Blewitt," says master, "I don't really understand what you mean."

"YOU DON'T KNOW WHAT I MEAN!" says Blewitt, in an axent such as I never before heard. "You don't know what I mean! Did you not promise me that we were to go shares? Didn't I lend you twenty sovereigns the other night to pay our losings to Dawkins? Didn't you swear, on your honor as a gentleman, to give me half of all that might be won in this affair?"

"Agreed, sir," says Deuceace; "agreed."

"Well, sir, and now what have you to say?"

"Why, THAT I DON'T INTEND TO KEEP MY PROMISE! You infernal fool and ninny! do you suppose I was laboring for YOU? Do you fancy I was going to the expense of giving a dinner to that jackass yonder, that you should profit by it? Get away, sir! Leave the room, sir! Or, stop—here—I will give you four hundred pounds—your own note of hand, sir, for that sum, if you will consent to forget all that has passed between us, and that you have never known Mr. Algernon Deuceace."

I've seen pipple angery before now, but never any like Blewitt. He stormed, groaned, belleod, swoar! At last, he fairly began blubbring; now cussing and nashing his teeth, now praying dear Mr. Deuceace to grant him mercy.

At last, master flung open the door (heaven bless us! it's well I didn't tumble hed over eels into the room!), and said, "Charles, show the gentleman down stairs!" My master looked at him quite steddy. Blewitt slunk down, as misrabble as any man I ever see. As for Dawkins, heaven knows where he was!

"Charles," says my master to me, about an hour afterwards, "I'm going to Paris; you may come, too, if you please."

FORING PARTS

It was a singular proof of my master's modesty, that though he had won this andsome sum of Mr. Dawkins, and was inclined to be as extravygant and osntatious as any man I ever seed, yet, when he determined on going to Paris, he didn't let a single frend know of all them winnings of his; didn't acquaint my Lord Crabs his father, that he was about to leave his natiff shoars—neigh—didn't even so much as call together his tradesmin, and pay off their little bills befor his departure.

On the contry, "Chawles," said he to me, "stick a piece of paper on my door," which is the way that lawyers do, "and write 'Back at seven' upon it." Back at seven I wrote, and stuck it on our outer oak. And so mistearus was Deuceace about his continental tour (to all except me), that when the landriss brought him her account for the last month (amountain, at the very least, to 2L. 10s.), master told her to leave it till Monday morning, when it should be properly settled. It's extrodny how ickonomical a man becomes, when he's got five thousand lbs. in his pockit.

Back at 7 indeed! At 7 we were a-roalin on the Dover Road, in the Reglator Coach—master inside, me out. A strange company of people there was, too, in that wehicle,—3 sailors; an Italyin with his music-box and munky; a missionary, going to convert the heathens in France; 2 oppra girls (they call 'em figure-aunts), and the figure-aunts' mothers inside; 4 Frenchmin, with gingybred caps and mustashes, singing, chattering, and jesticklating in the most vonderful vay. Such compliments as passed between them and the figure-aunts! such a munshin of biskits and sippin of brandy! such "O mong Jews," and "O sacrrres," and "kill fay frwaws!" I didn't understand their languidge at that time, so of course can't igsplain much of their conwersation; but it pleased me, nevertheless, for now I felt that I was reely going into foring parts: which, ever sins I had had any edication at all, was always my fondest wish. Heavin bless us! thought I, if these are specimeens of all Frenchmen, what a set they must be. The pore Italyin's monky, sittin mopin and meluncolly on his box, was not half so ugly, and seamed quite as reasonabble.

Well, we arrived at Dover—"Ship Hotel" weal cutlets half a ginny, glas of ale a shilling, glas of neagush, half a crownd, a hapnyworth of wax-lites four shillings, and so on. But master paid without grumbling; as long as it was for himself he never minded the expens: and nex day we embarked in the packit for Balong sir-mare—which means in French, the town of Balong sityouated on the sea. I who had heard of foring wonders, expected this to be the fust and greatest: phansy, then, my disapintment, when we got there, to find this Balong, not situated on the sea, but on the SHOAR.

But oh! the gettin there was the bisniss. How I did wish for Pump Court agin, as we were tawsing abowt in the Channel! Gentle reader, av you ever been on the otion?—"The sea, the sea, the open sea!" as Barry Cromwell says. As soon as we entered our little wessel, and I'd looked to master's luggitch and mine (mine was rapt up in a very small hankercher), as soon, I say, as we entered our little wessel, as soon as I saw the waives, black and frothy, like fresh drawn porter, a-dashin against the ribs of our galliant bark, the keal like a wedge, splittin the billoes in two, the sales a-flaffin in the hair, the standard of Hengland floating at the mask-head, the steward a-getting ready the basins and things, the capting proudly tredding the deck and giving orders to the salers, the white rox of Albany and the bathin-masheens disappearing in the distans—then, then I felt, for the first time, the mite, the madgisty of existence. "Yellowplush my boy," said I, in a dialogue with myself, "your life is now about to commens—your carear, as a man, dates from your entrans on board this packit. Be wise, be manly, be cautious, forgit the follies of your youth. You are no longer a boy now, but a FOOTMAN. Throw down your tops, your marbles, your boyish games—throw off your childish habbits with your inky clerk's jackit—throw up your—"

Here, I recklect, I was obleeged to stopp. A fealin, in the fust place singlar, in the next place painful, and at last compleatly overpowering, had come upon me while I was making the abuff speach, and now I found myself in a sityouation which Dellixy for Bids me to describe. Suffis to say, that now I dixcovered what basins was made for—that for many, many hours, I lay in a hagony of exostion, dead to all intense and porpuses, the rain pattering in my face, the salers tramplink over my body—the panes of purgatory going on inside. When we'd been about four hours in this sityouation (it seam'd to me four ears), the steward comes to that part of the deck where we servants were all huddled up together, and calls out "Charles!"

"Well," says I, gurgling out a faint "yes, what's the matter?"

"You're wanted."

"Where?"

"Your master's wery ill," says he, with a grin.

"Master be hanged!" says I, turning round, more misrable than ever. I woodn't have moved that day for twenty thousand masters—no, not for the Empror of Russia or the Pop of Room.

Well, to cut this sad subjik short, many and many a voyitch have I sins had upon what Shakspur calls the "wasty dip," but never such a retched one as that from Dover to Balong, in the year Anna Domino 1818. Steemers were scarce in those days; and our journey was made in a smack. At last, when I was in a stage of despare and exostion, as reely to phansy myself at Death's doar, we got to the end of our journey. Late in the evening we hailed the Gaelic shoars, and hankered in the arbor of Balong sir-mare.

It was the entrans of Parrowdice to me and master: and as we entered the calm water, and saw the comfrabble lights gleaming in the houses, and felt the roal of the vessel degreasing, never was two mortials gladder, I warrant, than we were. At length our capting drew up at the key, and our journey was down. But such a bustle and clatter, such jabbering, such shrieking and swaring, such wollies of oafs and axicrations as saluted us on landing, I never knew! We were boarded, in the fust place, by custom-house officers in cock-hats, who seased our luggitch, and called for our passpots: then a crowd of inn-waiters came, tumbling and screaming on deck—"Dis way, sare," cries one; "Hotel Meurice," says another; "Hotel de Bang," screeches another chap—the tower of Babyle was nothink to it. The fust thing that struck me on landing was a big fellow with ear-rings, who very nigh knock me down, in wrenching master's carpet-bag out of my hand, as I was carrying it to the hotell. But we got to it safe at last; and, for the fust time in my life, I slep in a foring country.

I shan't describe this town of Balong, which, as it has been visited by not less (on an avaridg) than two milliums of English since I fust saw it twenty years ago, is tolrabbly well known already. It's a dingy melumcolly place, to my mind; the only thing moving in the streets is the gutter which runs down 'em. As for wooden shoes, I saw few of 'em; and for frogs, upon my honor I never see a single Frenchman swallow one, which I had been led to beleave was their reg'lar, though beastly, custom. One thing which amazed me was the singlar name which they give to this town of Balong. It's divided, as every boddy knows, into an upper town (sitouate on a mounting, and surrounded by a wall, or bullyvar) and a lower town, which is on the level of the sea. Well, will it be believed that they call the upper town the Hot Veal, and the other the Base Veal, which is on the contry, genrally good in France, though the beaf, it must be confest, is excrabble.

It was in the Base Veal that Deuceace took his lodgian, at the Hotel de Bang, in a very crooked street called the Rue del Ascew; and if he'd been the Archbishop of Devonshire, or the Duke of Canterbury, he could not have given himself greater hairs, I can tell you. Nothink was too fine for us now; we had a sweet of rooms on the first floor, which belonged to the prime minister of France (at least the landlord said they were the premier's); and the Hon. Algernon Percy Deuceace, who had not paid his landriss, and came to Dover in a coach, seamed now to think that goold was too vulgar for him, and a carridge and six would break down with a man of his weight. Shampang flew about like ginger-pop, besides bordo, clarit, burgundy, burgong, and other wines, and all the delixes of the Balong kitchins. We stopped a fortnit at this dull place, and did nothing from morning till night excep walk on the bench, and watch the ships going in and out of arber, with one of them long, sliding opra-glasses, which they call, I don't know why, tallow-scoops. Our amusements for the fortnit we stopped here were boath numerous and daliteful; nothink, in fact, could be more pickong, as they say. In the morning before breakfast we boath walked on the Peer; master in a blue mareen jackit, and me in a slap-up new livry; both provided with long sliding opra-glasses, called as I said (I don't know Y, but I suppose it's a scientafick term) tallow-scoops. With these we igsamined, very attentively, the otion, the sea-weed, the pebbles, the dead cats, the fishwimmin, and the waives (like little children playing at leap-frog), which came tumblin over 1 another on to the shoar. It seemed to me as if they were scrambling to get there, as well they might, being sick of the sea, and anxious for the blessid, peaceable terry firmy.

After brexfast, down we went again (that is, master on his beat, and me on mine,—for my place in this foring town was a complete shinycure), and putting our tally-scoops again in our eyes, we egsamined a little more the otion, pebbils, dead cats, and so on; and this lasted till dinner, and dinner till bedtime, and bedtime lasted till nex day, when came brexfast, and dinner, and tally-scooping, as before. This is the way with all people of this town, of which, as I've heard say, there is ten thousand happy English, who lead this plesnt life from year's end to year's end.

Besides this, there's billiards and gambling for the gentlemen, a little dancing for the gals, and scandle for the dowygers. In none of these amusements did we partake. We were a LITTLE too good to play crown pints at cards, and never get paid when we won; or to go dangling after the portionless gals, or amuse ourselves with slops and penny-wist along with the old ladies. No, no; my master was a man of fortn now, and behayved himself as sich. If ever he condysended to go into the public room of the Hotel de Bang—the French (doubtless for reasons best known to themselves) call this a sallymanjy—he swoar more and lowder than any one there; he abyoused the waiters, the wittles, the wines. With his glas in his i, he staired at every body. He took always the place before the fire. He talked about "my carridge," "my currier," "my servant;" and he did wright. I've always found through life, that if you wish to be respected by English people, you must be insalent to them, especially if you are a sprig of nobiliaty. We LIKE being insulted by noblemen,—it shows they're familiar with us. Law bless us! I've known many and many a genlmn about town who'd rather be kicked by a lord than not be noticed by him; they've even had an aw of ME, because I was a lord's footman. While my master was hectoring in the parlor, at Balong, pretious airs I gave myself in the kitching, I can tell you; and the consequints was, that we were better served, and moar liked, than many pipple with twice our merit.

Deuceace had some particklar plans, no doubt, which kep him so long at Balong; and it clearly was his wish to act the man of fortune there for a little time before he tried the character of Paris. He purchased a carridge, he hired a currier, he rigged me in a fine new livry blazin with lace, and he past through the Balong bank a thousand pounds of the money he had won from Dawkins, to his credit at a Paris house; showing the Balong bankers at the same time, that he'd plenty moar in his potfolie. This was killin two birds with one stone; the bankers' clerks spread the nuse over the town, and in a day after master had paid the money every old dowyger in Balong had looked out the Crabs' family podigree in the Peeridge, and was quite intimate with the Deuceace name and estates. If Sattn himself were a lord, I do beleave there's many vurtuous English mothers would be glad to have him for a son-in-law.

Now, though my master had thought fitt to leave town without excommunicating with his father on the subject of his intended continental tripe, as soon as he was settled at Balong he roat my Lord Crabbs a letter, of which I happen to have a copy. It ran thus:—

"BOULOGNE, January 25.

"MY DEAR FATHER,—I have long, in the course of my legal studies, found the necessity of a knowledge of French, in which language all the early history of our profession is written, and have determined to take a little relaxation from chamber reading, which has seriously injured my health. If my modest finances can bear a two months' journey, and a residence at Paris, I propose to remain there that period.

"Will you have the kindness to send me a letter of introduction to Lord Bobtail, our ambassador? My name, and your old friendship with him, I know would secure me a reception at his house; but a pressing letter from yourself would at once be more courteous, and more effectual.

"May I also ask you for my last quarter's salary? I am not an expensive man, my dear father, as you know; but we are no chameleons, and fifty pounds (with my little earnings in my profession) would vastly add to the agremens of my continental excursion.

"Present my love to all my brothers and sisters. Ah! how I wish the hard portion of a younger son had not been mine, and that I could live without the dire necessity for labor, happy among the rural scenes of my childhood, and in the society of my dear sisters and you! Heaven bless you, dearest father, and all those beloved ones now dwelling under the dear old roof at Sizes.

"Ever your affectionate son,

"Algernon.

"THE RIGHT HON. THE EARL OF CRABS, &c.,

SIZES COURT, BUCKS."

To this affeckshnat letter his lordship replied, by return of poast, as follos:—

"MY DEAR ALGERNON,—Your letter came safe to hand and I enclose you the letter for Lord Bobtail as you desire. He is a kind man, and has one of the best cooks in Europe.

"We were all charmed with your warm remembrances of us, not having seen you for seven years. We cannot but be pleased at the family affection which, in spite of time and absence, still clings so fondly to home. It is a sad, selfish world, and very few who have entered it can afford to keep those fresh feelings which you have, my dear son.

"May you long retain them, is a fond father's earnest prayer. Be sure, dear Algernon, that they will be through life your greatest comfort, as well as your best worldly ally; consoling you in misfortune, cheering you in depression, aiding and inspiring you to exertion and success.

"I am sorry, truly sorry, that my account at Coutts's is so low, just now, as to render a payment of your allowance for the present impossible. I see by my book that I owe you now nine quarters, or 450L. Depend on it, my dear boy, that they shall be faithfully paid over to you on the first opportunity.

"By the way, I have enclosed some extracts from the newspapers, which may interest you: and have received a very strange letter from a Mr. Blewitt, about a play transaction, which, I suppose, is the case alluded to in these prints. He says you won 4700L. from one Dawkins: that the lad paid it; that he, Blewitt, was to go what he calls 'snacks' in the winning; but that you refused to share the booty. How can you, my dear boy, quarrel with these vulgar people, or lay yourself in any way open to their attacks? I have played myself a good deal, and there is no man living who can accuse me of a doubtful act. You should either have shot this Blewitt or paid him. Now, as the matter stands, it is too late to do the former; and, perhaps, it would be Quixotic to perform the latter. My dearest boy! recollect through life that YOU NEVER CAN AFFORD TO BE DISHONEST WITH A ROQUE. Four thousand seven hundred pounds was a great coup, to be sure.

"As you are now in such high feather, can you, dearest Algernon! lend me five hundred pounds? Upon my soul and honor, I will repay you. Your brothers and sisters send you their love. I need not add, that you have always the blessings of your affectionate father,

"CRABS."

"P.S.—Make it 500, and I will give you my note-of-hand for a thousand."

I needn't say that this did not QUITE enter into Deuceace's eyedears. Lend his father 500 pound, indeed! He'd as soon have lent him a box on the year! In the fust place, he hadn seen old Crabs for seven years, as that nobleman remarked in his epistol; in the secknd he hated him, and they hated each other; and nex, if master had loved his father ever so much, he loved somebody else better—his father's son, namely: and sooner than deprive that exlent young man of a penny, he'd have sean all the fathers in the world hangin at Newgat, and all the "beloved ones," as he called his sisters, the Lady Deuceacisses, so many convix at Bottomy Bay.

The newspaper parrografs showed that, however secret WE wished to keep the play transaction, the public knew it now full well. Blewitt, as I found after, was the author of the libels which appeared right and left:

"GAMBLING IN HIGH LIFE—the HONORABLE Mr. D—c—ce again!—This celebrated whist-player has turned his accomplishments to some profit. On Friday, the 16th January, he won five thousand pounds from a VERY young gentleman, Th—m—s Sm—th D—wk—ns, Esq., and lost two thousand five hundred to R. Bl-w-tt, Esq., of the T—mple. Mr. D. very honorably paid the sum lost by him to the honorable whist-player, but we have not heard that, BEFORE HIS SUDDEN TRIP TO PARIS, Mr. D—uc—ce paid HIS losings to Mr. Bl-w-tt."

Nex came a "Notice to Corryspondents:"

"Fair Play asks us, if we know of the gambling doings of the notorious Deuceace? We answer, WE DO; and, in our very next Number, propose to make some of them public."

They didn't appear, however; but, on the contry, the very same newspeper, which had been before so abusiff of Deuceace, was now loud in his praise. It said:—

"A paragraph was inadvertently admitted into our paper of last week, most unjustly assailing the character of a gentleman of high birth and talents, the son of the exemplary E-rl of Cr-bs. We repel, with scorn and indignation, the dastardly falsehoods of the malignant slanderer who vilified Mr. De—ce-ce, and beg to offer that gentleman the only reparation in our power for having thus tampered with his unsullied name. We disbelieve the RUFFIAN and HIS STORY, and most sincerely regret that such a tale, or SUCH A WRITER, should ever have been brought forward to the readers of this paper."

This was satisfactory, and no mistake: and much pleased we were at the denial of this conshentious editor. So much pleased that master sent him a ten-pound noat, and his complymints. He'd sent another to the same address, BEFORE this parrowgraff was printed; WHY, I can't think: for I woodn't suppose any thing musnary in a littery man.

Well, after this bisniss was concluded, the currier hired, the carridge smartened a little, and me set up in my new livries, we bade ojew to Bulong in the grandest state posbill. What a figure we cut! and, my i, what a figger the postillion cut! A cock-hat, a jackit made out of a cow's skin (it was in cold weather), a pig-tale about 3 fit in length, and a pair of boots! Oh, sich a pare! A bishop might almost have preached out of one, or a modrat-sized famly slep in it. Me and Mr. Schwigshhnaps, the currier, sate behind in the rumbill; master aloan in the inside, as grand as a Turk, and rapt up in his fine fir-cloak. Off we sett, bowing gracefly to the crowd; the harniss-bells jinglin, the great white hosses snortin, kickin, and squeelin, and the postilium cracking his wip, as loud as if he'd been drivin her majesty the quean.

Well, I shan't describe our voyitch. We passed sefral sitties, willitches, and metrappolishes; sleeping the fust night at Amiens, witch, as everyboddy knows, is famous ever since the year 1802 for what's called the Pease of Amiens. We had some, very good, done with sugar and brown sos, in the Amiens way. But after all the boasting about them, I think I like our marrowphats better.

Speaking of wedgytables, another singler axdent happened here concarning them. Master, who was brexfasting before going away, told me to go and get him his fur travling-shoes. I went and toald the waiter of the inn, who stared, grinned (as these chaps always do), said "Bong" (which means, very well), and presently came back.

I'M BLEST IF HE DIDN'T BRING MASTER A PLATE OF CABBITCH! Would you bleave it, that now, in the nineteenth sentry, when they say there's schoolmasters abroad, these stewpid French jackasses are so extonishingly ignorant as to call a CABBIDGE a SHOO! Never, never let it be said, after this, that these benighted, souperstitious, misrabble SAVIDGES, are equill, in any respex, to the great Brittish people. The moor I travvle, the moor I see of the world, and other natiums, I am proud of my own, and despise and deplore the retchid ignorance of the rest of Yourup.

My remarks on Parris you shall have by an early opportunity. Me and Deuceace played some curious pranx there, I can tell you.

CHAPTER I

THE TWO BUNDLES OF HAY

Lieutenant-General Sir George Griffin, K.C.B., was about seventy-five years old when he left this life, and the East Ingine army, of which he was a distinguished ornyment. Sir George's first appearance in Injar was in the character of a cabbingboy to a vessel; from which he rose to be clerk to the owners at Calcutta, from which he became all of a sudden a capting in the Company's service; and so rose and rose, until he rose to be a leftenant-general, when he stopped rising altogether—hopping the twig of this life, as drummers, generals, dustmen, and emperors must do.

Sir George did not leave any mal hair to perpetuate the name of Griffin. A widow of about twenty-seven, and a daughter avaritching twenty-three, was left behind to deploar his loss, and share his proppaty. On old Sir George's deth, his interesting widdo and orfan, who had both been with him in Injer, returned home—tried London for a few months, did not like it, and resolved on a trip to Paris; where very small London people become very great ones, if they've money, as these Griffinses had. The intelligent reader need not be told that Miss Griffin was not the daughter of Lady Griffin; for though marritches are made tolrabbly early in Injer, people are not quite so precoashoos as all that: the fact is, Lady G. was Sir George's second wife. I need scarcely add, that Miss Matilda Griffin wos the offspring of his fust marritch.

Miss Leonora Kicksey, a ansum, lively Islington gal, taken out to Calcutta, and, amongst his other goods, very comfortably disposed of by her uncle, Capting Kicksey, was one-and-twenty when she married Sir George at seventy-one; and the 13 Miss Kickseys, nine of whom kep a school at Islington (the other 4 being married variously in the city), were not a little envius of my lady's luck, and not a little proud of their relationship to her. One of 'em, Miss Jemima Kicksey, the oldest, and by no means the least ugly of the sett, was staying with her ladyship, and gev me all the partecklars. Of the rest of the famly, being of a lo sort, I in course no nothink; MY acquaintance, thank my stars, don't lie among them, or the likes of them.

Well, this Miss Jemima lived with her younger and more fortnat sister, in the qualaty of companion, or toddy. Poar thing! I'd a soon be a gally slave, as lead the life she did! Every body in the house despised her; her ladyship insulted her; the very kitching gals scorned and flouted her. She roat the notes, she kep the bills, she made the tea, she whipped the chocklate, she cleaned the canary birds, and gev out the linning for the wash. She was my lady's walking pocket, or rettycule; and fetched and carried her handkercher, or her smell-bottle, like a well-bred spaniel. All night, at her ladyship's swarries, she thumped kidrills (nobody ever thought of asking HER to dance!); when Miss Griffing sung, she played the piano, and was scolded because the singer was out of tune; abommanating dogs, she never drove out without her ladyship's puddle in her lap; and, reglarly unwell in a carriage, she never got anything but the back seat. Poar Jemima! I can see her now in my lady's SECKND-BEST old clothes (the ladies'-maids always got the prime leavings): a liloc sattn gown, crumpled, blotched, and greasy; a pair of white sattn shoes, of the color of Inger rubber; a faded yellow velvet hat, with a wreath of hartifishl flowers run to sead, and a bird of Parrowdice perched on the top of it, melumcolly and moulting, with only a couple of feathers left in his unfortunate tail.

Besides this ornyment to their saloon, Lady and Miss Griffin kept a number of other servants in the kitching; 2 ladies'-maids; 2 footmin, six feet high each, crimson coats, goold knots, and white cassymear pantyloons; a coachmin to match; a page: and a Shassure, a kind of servant only known among forriners, and who looks more like a major-general than any other mortial, wearing a cock-hat, a unicorn covered with silver lace, mustashos, eplets, and a sword by his side. All these to wait upon two ladies; not counting a host of the fair sex, such as cooks, scullion, housekeepers, and so forth.

My Lady Griffin's lodging was at forty pound a week, in a grand sweet of rooms in the Plas Vandome at Paris. And, having thus described their house, and their servants' hall, I may give a few words of description concerning the ladies themselves.

In the fust place, and in coarse, they hated each other. My lady was twenty-seven—a widdo of two years—fat, fair, and rosy. A slow, quiet, cold-looking woman, as those fair-haired gals generally are, it seemed difficult to rouse her either into likes or dislikes; to the former, at least. She never loved any body but ONE, and that was herself. She hated, in her calm, quiet way, almost every one else who came near her—every one, from her neighbor, the duke, who had slighted her at dinner, down to John the footman, who had torn a hole in her train. I think this woman's heart was like one of them lithograffic stones, you CAN'T RUB OUT ANY THING when once it's drawn or wrote on it; nor could you out of her ladyship's stone—heart, I mean—in the shape of an affront, a slight, or real, or phansied injury. She boar an exlent, irreprotchable character, against which the tongue of scandal never wagged. She was allowed to be the best wife posbill—and so she was; but she killed her old husband in two years, as dead as ever Mr. Thurtell killed Mr. William Weare. She never got into a passion, not she—she never said a rude word; but she'd a genius—a genius which many women have—of making A HELL of a house, and tort'ring the poor creatures of her family, until they were wellnigh drove mad.

Miss Matilda Griffin was a good deal uglier, and about as amiable as her mother-in-law. She was crooked, and squinted; my lady, to do her justice, was straight, and looked the same way with her i's. She was dark, and my lady was fair—sentimental, as her ladyship was cold. My lady was never in a passion—Miss Matilda always; and awfille were the scenes which used to pass between these 2 women, and the wickid, wickid quarls which took place. Why did they live together? There was the mistry. Not related, and hating each other like pison, it would surely have been easier to remain seprat, and so have detested each other at a distans.

As for the fortune which old Sir George had left, that, it was clear, was very considrabble—300 thousand lb. at the least, as I have heard say. But nobody knew how it was disposed of. Some said that her ladyship was sole mistriss of it, others that it was divided, others that she had only a life inkum, and that the money was all to go (as was natral) to Miss Matilda. These are subjix which are not praps very interesting to the British public, but were mighty important to my master, the Honrable Algernon Percy Deuceace, esquire, barrister-at-law, etsettler, etsettler.

For I've forgot to inform you that my master was very intimat in this house; and that we were now comfortably settled at the Hotel Mirabew (pronounced Marobo in French), in the Rew delly Pay, at Paris. We had our cab, and two riding horses; our banker's book, and a thousand pound for a balantz at Lafitt's; our club at the corner of the Rew Gramong; our share in a box at the oppras; our apartments, spacious and elygant; our swarries at court; our dinners at his excellency Lord Bobtail's and elsewhere. Thanks to poar Dawkins's five thousand pound, we were as complete gentlemen as any in Paris.

Now my master, like a wise man as he was, seaing himself at the head of a smart sum of money, and in a country where his debts could not bother him, determined to give up for the present every think like gambling—at least, high play; as for losing or winning a ralow of Napoleums at whist or ecarty, it did not matter; it looks like money to do such things, and gives a kind of respectabilaty. "But as for play, he wouldn't—oh no! not for worlds!—do such a thing." He HAD played, like other young men of fashn, and won and lost [old fox! he didn't say he had PAID]; but he had given up the amusement, and was now determined, he said, to live on his inkum. The fact is, my master was doing his very best to act the respectable man: and a very good game it is, too; but it requires a precious great roag to play it.

He made his appearans reglar at church—me carrying a handsome large black marocky Prayer-book and Bible, with the psalms and lessons marked out with red ribbings; and you'd have thought, as I graivly laid the volloms down before him, and as he berried his head in his nicely brushed hat, before service began, that such a pious, proper morl, young nobleman was not to be found in the whole of the peeridge. It was a comfort to look at him. Efry old tabby and dowyger at my Lord Bobtail's turned up the wights of their i's when they spoke of him, and vowed they had never seen such a dear, daliteful, exlent young man. What a good son he must be, they said; and oh, what a good son-in-law! He had the pick of all the English gals at Paris before we had been there 3 months. But, unfortunately, most of them were poar; and love and a cottidge was not quite in master's way of thinking.

Well, about this time my Lady Griffin and Miss G. made their appearans at Parris, and master, who was up to snough, very soon changed his noat. He sate near them at chapple, and sung hims with my lady: he danced with 'em at the embassy balls; he road with them in the Boy de Balong and the Shandeleasies (which is the French High Park); he roat potry in Miss Griffin's halbim, and sang jewets along with her and Lady Griffin; he brought sweet-meats for the puddle-dog; he gave money to the footmin, kissis and gloves to the sniggering ladies'-maids; he was sivvle even to poar Miss Kicksey; there wasn't a single soal at the Griffinses that didn't adoar this good young man.

The ladies, if they hated befoar, you may be sure detested each other now wuss than ever. There had been always a jallowsy between them: miss jellows of her mother-in-law's bewty; madam of miss's espree: miss taunting my lady about the school at Islington, and my lady sneering at miss for her squint and her crookid back. And now came a stronger caws. They both fell in love with Mr. Deuceace—my lady, that is to say, as much as she could, with her cold selfish temper. She liked Deuceace, who amused her and made her laff. She liked his manners, his riding, and his good loox; and being a pervinew herself had a dubble respect for real aristocratick flesh and blood. Miss's love, on the contry, was all flams and fury. She'd always been at this work from the time she had been at school, where she very nigh run away with a Frentch master; next with a footman (which I may say, in confidence, is by no means unnatral or unusyouall, as I COULD SHOW IF I LIKED); and so had been going on sins fifteen. She reglarly flung herself at Deuceace's head—such sighing, crying, and ogling, I never see. Often was I ready to bust out laffin, as I brought master skoars of rose-colored billydoos, folded up like cockhats, and smellin like barber's shops, which this very tender young lady used to address to him. Now, though master was a scoundrill and no mistake, he was a gentlemin, and a man of good breading; and miss CAME A LITTLE TOO STRONG (pardon the wulgarity of the xpression) with her hardor and attachmint, for one of his taste. Besides, she had a crookid spine, and a squint; so that (supposing their fortns tolrabbly equal) Deuceace reely preferred the mother-in-law.

Now, then, it was his bisniss to find out which had the most money. With an English famly this would have been easy: a look at a will at Doctor Commons'es would settle the matter at once. But this India naybob's will was at Calcutty, or some outlandish place; and there was no getting sight of a coppy of it. I will do Mr. Algernon Deuceace the justass to say, that he was so little musnary in his love for Lady Griffin, that he would have married her gladly, even if she had ten thousand pounds less than Miss Matilda. In the meantime, his plan was to keep 'em both in play, until he could strike the best fish of the two—not a difficult matter for a man of his genus: besides, Miss was hooked for certain.

CHAPTER II

"HONOR THY FATHER"

I said that my master was adoard by every person in my Lady Griffin's establishmint. I should have said by every person excep one,—a young French gnlmn, that is, who, before our appearants, had been mighty partiklar with my lady, ockupying by her side exackly the same pasition which the Honrable Mr. Deuceace now held. It was bewtiffle and headifying to see how coolly that young nobleman kicked the poar Shevalliay de L'Orge out of his shoes, and how gracefully he himself stept into 'em. Munseer de L'Orge was a smart young French jentleman, of about my master's age and good looks, but not possest of half my master's impidence. Not that that quallaty is uncommon in France; but few, very few, had it to such a degree as my exlent employer, Mr. Deuceace. Besides De L'Orge was reglarly and reely in love with Lady Griffin, and master only pretending: he had, of coars, an advantitch, which the poor Frentchman never could git. He was all smiles and gaty, while Delorge was ockward and melumcolly. My master had said twenty pretty things to Lady Griffin, befor the shevalier had finished smoothing his hat, staring at her, and sighing fit to bust his weskit. O luv, luv! THIS isn't the way to win a woman, or my name's not Fitzroy Yellowplush! Myself, when I begun my carear among the fair six, I was always sighing and moping, like this poar Frenchman. What was the consquints? The foar fust women I adoared lafft at me, and left me for something more lively. With the rest I have edopted a diffrent game, and with tolerable suxess, I can tell you. But this is eggatism, which I aboar.

Well, the long and the short of it is, that Munseer Ferdinand Hyppolite Xavier Stanislas, Shevalier de L'Orge, was reglar cut out by Munseer Algernon Percy Deuceace, Exquire. Poar Ferdinand did not leave the house—he hadn't the heart to do that—nor had my lady the desire to dismiss him. He was usefle in a thousand different ways, gitting oppra-boxes, and invitations to French swarries, bying gloves, and O de Colong, writing French noats, and such like. Always let me recommend an English famly, going to Paris, to have at least one young man of the sort about them. Never mind how old your ladyship is, he will make love to you; never mind what errints you send him upon, he'll trot off and do them. Besides, he's always quite and well-dresst, and never drinx moar than a pint of wine at dinner, which (as I say) is a pint to consider. Such a conveniants of a man was Munseer de L'Orge—the greatest use and comfort to my lady posbill; if it was but to laff at his bad pronunciatium of English, it was somethink amusink; the fun was to pit him against poar Miss Kicksey, she speakin French, and he our naytif British tong.

My master, to do him justace, was perfickly sivvle to this poar young Frenchman; and having kicked him out of the place which he occupied, sertingly treated his fallen anymy with every respect and consideration. Poar modist, down-hearted little Ferdinand adoured my lady as a goddice! and so he was very polite likewise to my master—never venturing once to be jellows of him, or to question my Lady Griffin's right to change her lover, if she choase to do so.

Thus, then, matters stood; master had two strinx to his bo, and might take either the widdo or the orfn, as he preferred: com bong lwee somblay, as the Frentch say. His only pint was to discover how the money was disposed off, which evidently belonged to one or other, or boath. At any rate he was sure of one; as sure as any mortal man can be in this sublimary spear, where nothink is suttin except unsertnty.

A very unixpected insident here took place, which in a good deal changed my master's calkylations.

One night, after conducting the two ladies to the oppra, after suppink of white soop, sammy-deperdrow, and shampang glassy (which means eyced), at their house in the Plas Vandom, me and master droav hoam in the cab, as happy as possbill.

"Chawls you damned scoundrel," says he to me (for he was in an exlent humer), "when I'm married, I'll dubbil your wagis."

This he might do, to be sure, without injuring himself, seeing that he had us yet never paid me any. But, what then? Law bless us! things would be at a pretty pass if we suvvants only lived on our WAGIS; our puckwisits is the thing, and no mistake.

I ixprest my gratitude as best I could; swoar that it wasn't for wagis I served him—that I would as leaf weight upon him for nothink; and that never, never, so long as I livd, would I, of my own accord, part from such an exlent master. By the time these two spitches had been made—my spitch and his—we arrived at the "Hotel Mirabeu;" which, us every body knows, ain't very distant from the Plas Vandome. Up we marched to our apartmince, me carrying the light and the cloax, master hummink a hair out of the oppra, as merry as a lark.

I opened the door of our salong. There was lights already in the room; an empty shampang bottle roalin on the floar, another on the table; near which the sofy was drawn, and on it lay a stout old genlmn, smoaking seagars as if he'd bean in an inn tap-room.

Deuceace (who abommunates seagars, as I've already shown) bust into a furious raige against the genlmn, whom he could hardly see for the smoak; and, with a number of oaves quite unnecessary to repeat, asked him what bisniss he'd there.

The smoaking chap rose, and, laying down his seagar, began a ror of laffin, and said, "What! Algy my boy! don't you know me?"

The reader may praps recklect a very affecting letter which was published in the last chapter of these memoars; in which the writer requested a loan of five hundred pound from Mr. Algernon Deuceace, and which boar the respected signatur of the Earl of Crabs, Mr. Deuceace's own father. It was that distinguished arastycrat who was now smokin and laffin in our room.

My Lord Crabs was, as I preshumed, about 60 years old. A stowt, burly, red-faced, bald-headed nobleman, whose nose seemed blushing at what his mouth was continually swallowing; whose hand, praps, trembled a little; and whose thy and legg was not quite so full or as steddy as they had been in former days. But he was a respecktabble, fine-looking old nobleman; and though it must be confest, 1/2 drunk when we fust made our appearance in the salong, yet by no means moor so than a reel noblemin ought to be.

"What, Algy my boy!" shouts out his lordship, advancing and seasing master by the hand, "doan't you know your own father?"

Master seemed anythink but overhappy. "My lord," says he, looking very pail, and speakin rayther slow, "I didn't—I confess—the unexpected pleasure—of seeing you in Paris. The fact is, sir, said he," recovering himself a little; "the fact is, there was such a confounded smoke of tobacco in the room, that I really could not see who the stranger was who had paid me such an unexpected visit."

"A bad habit, Algernon; a bad habit," said my lord, lighting another seagar: "a disgusting and filthy practice, which you, my dear child, will do well to avoid. It is at best, dear Algernon, but a nasty, idle pastime, unfitting a man as well for mental exertion as for respectable society; sacrificing, at once, the vigor of the intellect and the graces of the person. By-the-by, what infernal bad tobacco they have, too, in this hotel. Could not you send your servant to get me a few seagars at the Cafe de Paris? Give him a five-franc piece, and let him go at once, that's a good fellow."

Here his lordship hiccupt, and drank off a fresh tumbler of shampang. Very sulkily, master drew out the coin, and sent me on the errint.

Knowing the Cafe de Paris to be shut at that hour, I didn't say a word, but quietly establisht myself in the ante-room; where, as it happened by a singler coinstdints, I could hear every word of the conversation between this exlent pair of relatifs.

"Help yourself, and get another bottle," says my lord, after a sollum paws. My poar master, the king of all other compnies in which he moved, seamed here but to play secknd fiddill, and went to the cubbard, from which his father had already igstracted two bottils of his prime Sillary.

He put it down before his father, coft, spit, opened the windows, stirred the fire, yawned, clapt his hand to his forehead, and suttnly seamed as uneezy as a genlmn could be. But it was of no use; the old one would not budg. "Help yourself," says he again, "and pass me the bottil."

"You are very good, father," says master; "but really, I neither drink nor smoke."

"Right, my boy: quite right. Talk about a good conscience in this life—a good STOMACK is everythink. No bad nights, no headachs—eh? Quite cool and collected for your law studies in the morning?—eh?" And the old nobleman here grinned, in a manner which would have done creddit to Mr. Grimoldi.

Master sate pale and wincing, as I've seen a pore soldier under the cat. He didn't anser a word. His exlent pa went on, warming as he continued to speak, and drinking a fresh glas at evry full stop.

"How you must improve, with such talents and such principles! Why, Algernon, all London talks of your industry and perseverance: you're not merely a philosopher, man; hang it! you've got the philosopher's stone. Fine rooms, fine horses, champagne, and all for 200 a year!"

"I presume, sir," says my master, "that you mean the two hundred a year which YOU pay me?"

"The very sum, my boy; the very sum!" cries my lord, laffin as if he would die. "Why, that's the wonder! I never pay the two hundred a year, and you keep all this state up upon nothing. Give me your secret, O you young Trismegistus! Tell your old father how such wonders can be worked, and I will—yes, then, upon my word, I will—pay you your two hundred a year!"

"Enfin, my lord," says Mr. Deuceace, starting up, and losing all patience, "will you have the goodness to tell me what this visit means? You leave me to starve, for all you care; and you grow mighty facetious because I earn my bread. You find me in prosperity, and—"

"Precisely, my boy; precisely. Keep your temper, and pass that bottle. I find you in prosperity; and a young gentleman of your genius and acquirements asks me why I seek your society? Oh, Algernon! Algernon! this is not worthy of such a profound philosopher. WHY do I seek you? Why, because you ARE in prosperity, O my son! else, why the devil should I bother my self about you? Did I, your poor mother, or your family, ever get from you a single affectionate feeling? Did we, or any other of your friends or intimates, ever know you to be guilty of a single honest or generous action? Did we ever pretend any love for you, or you for us? Algernon Deuceace, you don't want a father to tell you that you are a swindler and a spendthrift! I have paid thousands for the debts of yourself and your brothers; and, if you pay nobody else, I am determined you shall repay me. You would not do it by fair means, when I wrote to you and asked you for a loan of money. I knew you would not. Had I written again to warn you of my coming, you would have given me the slip; and so I came, uninvited, to FORCE you to repay me. THAT'S why I am here, Mr. Algernon; and so help yourself and pass the bottle."

After this speach, the old genlmn sunk down on the sofa, and puffed as much smoke out of his mouth as if he'd been the chimley of a steam-injian. I was pleased, I confess, with the sean, and liked to see this venrabble and virtuous old man a-nocking his son about the hed; just as Deuceace had done with Mr. Richard Blewitt, as I've before shown. Master's face was, fust, red-hot; next, chawk-white: and then sky-blew. He looked, for all the world, like Mr. Tippy Cooke in the tragady of Frankinstang. At last, he mannidged to speek.

"My lord," says he, "I expected when I saw you that some such scheme was on foot. Swindler and spendthrift as I am, at least it is but a family failing; and I am indebted for my virtues to my father's precious example. Your lordship has, I perceive, added drunkenness to the list of your accomplishments, and, I suppose, under the influence of that gentlemanly excitement, has come to make these preposterous propositions to me. When you are sober, you will, perhaps, be wise enough to know, that, fool as I may be, I am not such a fool as you think me; and that if I have got money, I intend to keep it—every farthing of it, though you were to be ten times as drunk, and ten times as threatening as you are now."

"Well, well, my boy," said Lord Crabs, who seemed to have been half asleep during his son's oratium, and received all his sneers and surcasms with the most complete good-humor; "well, well, if you will resist, tant pis pour toi. I've no desire to ruin you, recollect, and am not in the slightest degree angry but I must and will have a thousand pounds. You had better give me the money at once; it will cost you more if you don't."

"Sir," says Mr. Deuceace, "I will be equally candid. I would not give you a farthing to save you from—"

Here I thought proper to open the doar, and, touching my hat, said, "I have been to the Cafe de Paris, my lord, but the house is shut."

"Bon: there's a good lad; you may keep the five francs. And now, get me a candle and show me down stairs."

But my master seized the wax taper. "Pardon me, my lord," says he. "What! a servant do it, when your son is in the room? Ah, par exemple, my dear father," said he, laughing, "you think there is no politeness left among us." And he led the way out.

"Good night, my dear boy," said Lord Crabs.

"God bless you, sir," says he. "Are you wrapped warm? Mind the step!"

And so this affeckshnate pair parted.

CHAPTER III

MINEWVRING

Master rose the nex morning with a dismal countinants—he seamed to think that his pa's visit boded him no good. I heard him muttering at his brexfast, and fumbling among his hundred pound notes; once he had laid a parsle of them aside (I knew what he meant), to send 'em to his father. "But no," says he at last, clutching them all up together again, and throwing them into his escritaw, "what harm can he do me? If he is a knave, I know another who's full as sharp. Let's see if we cannot beat him at his own weapons." With that Mr. Deuceace drest himself in his best clothes, and marched off to the Plas Vandom, to pay his cort to the fair widdo and the intresting orfn.

It was abowt ten o'clock, and he proposed to the ladies, on seeing them, a number of planns for the day's rackryation. Riding in the Body Balong, going to the Twillaries to see King Looy Disweet (who was then the raining sufferin of the French crownd) go to chapple, and, finely, a dinner at 5 o'clock at the Caffy de Parry; whents they were all to adjourn, to see a new peace at the theatre of the Pot St. Martin, called Sussannar and the Elders.

The gals agread to everythink, exsep the two last prepositiums. "We have an engagement, my dear Mr. Algernon," said my lady. "Look—a very kind letter from Lady Bobtail." And she handed over a pafewmd noat from that exolted lady. It ran thus:—

"FBG. ST. HONORE, Thursday, Feb. 15, 1817.

"MY DEAR LADY GRIFFIN,—It is an age since we met. Harassing public duties occupy so much myself and Lord Bobtail, that we have scarce time to see our private friends; among whom, I hope, my dear Lady Griffin will allow me to rank her. Will you excuse so unceremonious an invitation, and dine with us at the embassy to-day? We shall be en petite comite, and shall have the pleasure of hearing, I hope, some of your charming daughter's singing in the evening. I ought, perhaps, to have addressed a separate, note to dear Miss Griffin; but I hope she will pardon a poor diplomate, who has so many letters to write, you know.

"Farewell till seven, when I POSITIVELY MUST see you both. Ever, dearest Lady Griffin, your affectionate

"ELIZA BOBTAIL."

Such a letter from the ambassdriss, brot by the ambasdor's Shassure, and sealed with his seal of arms, would affect anybody in the middling ranx of life. It droav Lady Griffin mad with delight; and, long before my master's arrivle, she'd sent Mortimer and Fitzclarence, her two footmin, along with a polite reply in the affummatiff.

Master read the noat with no such fealinx of joy. He felt that there was somethink a-going on behind the seans, and, though he could not tell how, was sure that some danger was near him. That old fox of a father of his had begun his M'Inations pretty early!

Deuceace handed back the letter; sneared, and poohd, and hinted that such an invitation was an insult at best (what he called a pees ally); and, the ladies might depend upon it, was only sent because Lady Bobtail wanted to fill up two spare places at her table. But Lady Griffin and Miss would not have his insinwations; they knew too fu lords ever to refuse an invitatium from any one of them. Go they would; and poor Deuceace must dine alone. After they had been on their ride, and had had their other amusemince, master came back with them, chatted, and laft; he was mighty sarkastix with my lady; tender and sentrymentle with Miss; and left them both in high sperrits to perform their twollet, before dinner.

As I came to the door (for I was as famillyer as a servnt of the house), as I came into the drawing-room to announts his cab, I saw master very quietly taking his pocket-book (or pot fool, as the French call it) and thrusting it under one of the cushinx of the sofa. What game is this? thinx I.

Why, this was the game. In abowt two hours, when he knew the ladies were gon, he pretends to be vastly anxious abowt the loss of his potfolio; and back he goes to Lady Griffinses to seek for it there.

"Pray," says he, on going in, "ask Miss Kicksey if I may see her for a single moment." And down comes Miss Kicksey, quite smiling, and happy to see him.

"Law, Mr. Deuceace!" says she, trying to blush as hard as ever she could, "you quite surprise me! I don't know whether I ought, really, being alone, to admit a gentleman."

"Nay, don't say so, dear Miss Kicksey! for do you know, I came here for a double purpose—to ask about a pocket-book which I have lost, and may, perhaps, have left here; and then, to ask you if you will have the great goodness to pity a solitary bachelor, and give him a cup of your nice tea?"

NICE TEA! I thot I should have split; for I'm blest if master had eaten a morsle of dinner!

Never mind: down to tea they sat. "Do you take cream and sugar, dear sir?" says poar Kicksey, with a voice as tender as a tuttle-duff.

"Both, dearest Miss Kicksey!" answers master; who stowed in a power of sashong and muffinx which would have done honor to a washawoman.

I shan't describe the conversation that took place betwigst master and this young lady. The reader, praps, knows y Deuceace took the trouble to talk to her for an hour, and to swallow all her tea. He wanted to find out from her all she knew about the famly money matters, and settle at once which of the two Griffinses he should marry.

The poar thing, of cors, was no match for such a man as my master. In a quarter of an hour, he had, if I may use the igspression, "turned her inside out." He knew everything that she knew; and that, poar creature, was very little. There was nine thousand a year, she had heard say, in money, in houses, in banks in Injar, and what not. Boath the ladies signed papers for selling or buying, and the money seemed equilly divided betwigst them.

NINE THOUSAND A YEAR! Deuceace went away, his cheex tingling, his heart beating. He, without a penny, could nex morning, if he liked, be master of five thousand per hannum!

Yes. But how? Which had the money, the mother or the daughter? All the tea-drinking had not taught him this piece of nollidge; and Deuceace thought it a pity that he could not marry both.

The ladies came back at night, mightaly pleased with their reception at the ambasdor's; and, stepping out of their carridge, bid coachmin drive on with a gentlemin who had handed them out—a stout old gentlemin, who shook hands most tenderly at parting, and promised to call often upon my Lady Griffin. He was so polite, that he wanted to mount the stairs with her ladyship; but no, she would not suffer it. "Edward," says she to the coachmin, quite loud, and pleased that all the people in the hotel should hear her, "you will take the carriage, and drive HIS LORDSHIP home." Now, can you guess who his lordship was? The Right Hon. the Earl of Crabs, to be sure; the very old genlmn whom I had seen on such charming terms with his son the day before. Master knew this the nex day, and began to think he had been a fool to deny his pa the thousand pound.

Now, though the suckmstansies of the dinner at the ambasdor's only came to my years some time after, I may as well relate 'em here, word for word, as they was told me by the very genlmn who waited behind Lord Crabseses chair.

There was only a "petty comity" at dinner, as Lady Bobtail said; and my Lord Crabs was placed betwigst the two Griffinses, being mighty ellygant and palite to both. "Allow me," says he to Lady G. (between the soop and the fish), "my dear madam, to thank you—fervently thank you for your goodness to my poor boy. Your ladyship is too young to experience, but, I am sure, far too tender not to understand the gratitude which must fill a fond parent's heart for kindness shown to his child. Believe me," says my lord, looking her full and tenderly in the face, "that the favors you have done to another have been done equally to myself, and awaken in my bosom the same grateful and affectionate feelings with which you have already inspired my son Algernon."

Lady Griffin blusht, and droopt her head till her ringlets fell into her fish-plate: and she swallowed Lord Crabs's flumry just as she would so many musharuins. My lord (whose powers of slack-jaw was notoarious) nex addrast another spitch to Miss Griffin. He said he'd heard how Deuceace was SITUATED. Miss blusht—what a happy dog he was—Miss blusht crimson, and then he sighed deeply, and began eating his turbat and lobster sos. Master was a good un at flumry, but, law bless you! he was no moar equill to the old man than a mole-hill is to a mounting. Before the night was over, he had made as much progress as another man would in a ear. One almost forgot his red nose and his big stomick, and his wicked leering i's, in his gentle insiniwating woice, his fund of annygoats, and, above all, the bewtific, morl, religious, and honrabble toan of his genral conservation. Praps you will say that these ladies were, for such rich pipple, mightaly esaly captivated; but recklect, my dear sir, that they were fresh from

Injar,—that they'd not sean many lords,—that they adoared the peeridge, as every honest woman does in England who has proper feelinx, and has read the fashnabble novvles,—and that here at Paris was their fust step into fashnabble sosiaty.

Well, after dinner, while Miss Matilda was singing "Die tantie," or "Dip your chair," or some of them sellabrated Italyian hairs (when she began this squall, hang me if she'd ever stop), my lord gets hold of Lady Griffin again, and gradgaly begins to talk to her in a very different strane.

"What a blessing it is for us all," says he, "that Algernon has found a friend so respectable as your ladyship."

"Indeed, my lord; and why? I suppose I am not the only respectable friend that Mr. Deuceace has?"

"No, surely; not the only one he HAS HAD: his birth, and, permit me to say, his relationship to myself, have procured him many. But—" (here my lord heaved a very affecting and large sigh).

"But what?" says my lady, laffing at the igspression of his dismal face. "You don't mean that Mr. Deuceace has lost them or is unworthy of them?"

"I trust not, my dear madam, I trust not; but he is wild, thoughtless, extravagant, and embarrassed: and you know a man under these circumstances is not very particular as to his associates."

"Embarrassed? Good heavens! He says he has two thousand a year left him by a god-mother; and he does not seem even to spend his income—a very handsome independence, too, for a bachelor."

My lord nodded his head sadly, and said,—"Will your ladyship give me your word of honor to be secret? My son has but a thousand a year, which I allow him, and is heavily in debt. He has played, madam, I fear; and for this reason I am so glad to hear that he is in a respectable domestic circle, where he may learn, in the presence of far greater and purer attractions, to forget the dice-box, and the low company which has been his bane."

My Lady Griffin looked very grave indeed. Was it true? Was Deuceace sincere in his professions of love, or was he only a sharper wooing her for her money? Could she doubt her informer? his own father, and, what's more, a real flesh and blood pear of parlyment? She determined she would try him. Praps she did not know she had liked Deuceace so much, until she kem to feel how much she should HATE him if she found he'd been playing her false.

The evening was over, and back they came, as wee've seen,—my lord driving home in my lady's carridge, her ladyship and Miss walking up stairs to their own apartmince.

Here, for a wonder, was poar Miss Kicksey quite happy and smiling, and evidently full of a secret,—something mighty pleasant, to judge from her loox. She did not long keep it. As she was making tea for the ladies (for in that house they took a cup regular before bedtime), "Well, my lady," says she, "who do you think has been to drink tea with me?" Poar thing, a frendly face was an event in her life—a tea-party quite a hera!

"Why, perhaps, Lenoir my maid," says my lady, looking grave. "I wish, Miss Kicksey, you would not demean yourself by mixing with my domestics. Recollect, madam, that you are sister to Lady Griffin."

"No, my lady, it was not Lenoir; it was a gentleman, and a handsome gentleman, too."

"Oh, it was Monsieur de l'Orge, then," says Miss; "he promised to bring me some guitar-strings."

"No, nor yet M. de l'Orge. He came, but was not so polite as to ask for me. What do you think of your own beau, the Honorable Mr. Algernon Deuceace;" and, so saying, poar Kicksey clapped her hands together, and looked as joyfle as if she'd come in to a fortin.

"Mr. Deuceace here; and why, pray?" says my lady, who recklected all that his exlent pa had been saying to her.

"Why, in the first place, he had left his pocket-book, and in the second, he wanted, he said, a dish of my nice tea; which he took, and stayed with me an hour, or moar."

"And pray, Miss Kicksey," said Miss Matilda, quite contempshusly, "what may have been the subject of your conversation with Mr. Algernon? Did you talk politics, or music, or fine arts, or metaphysics?" Miss M. being what was called a blue (as most hump-backed women in sosiaty are), always made a pint to speak on these grand subjects.

"No, indeed; he talked of no such awful matters. If he had, you know, Matilda, I should never have understood him. First we talked about the weather, next about muffins and crumpets. Crumpets, he said, he liked best; and then we talked" (here Miss Kicksey's voice fell) "about poor dear Sir George in heaven! what a good husband he was, and—"

"What a good fortune he left, eh, Miss Kicksey?" says my lady, with a hard, snearing voice, and a diabollicle grin.

"Yes, dear Leonora, he spoke so respectfully of your blessed husband, and seemed so anxious about you and Matilda, it was quite charming to hear him, dear man!"

"And pray, Miss Kicksey, what did you tell him?"

"Oh, I told him that you and Leonora had nine thousand a year, and—"

"What then?"

"Why, nothing; that is all I know. I am sure I wish I had ninety," says poor Kicksey, her eyes turning to heaven.

"Ninety fiddlesticks! Did not Mr. Deuceace ask how the money was left, and to which of us?"

"Yes; but I could not tell him."

"I knew it!" says my lady, slapping down her tea-cup,—"I knew it!"

"Well!" says Miss Matilda, "and why not, Lady Griffin? There is no reason you should break your tea-cup, because Algernon asks a harmless question. HE is not mercenary; he is all candor, innocence, generosity!

He is himself blessed with a sufficient portion of the world's goods to be content; and often and often has he told me he hoped the woman of his choice might come to him without a penny, that he might show the purity of his affection."

"I've no doubt," says my lady. "Perhaps the lady of his choice is Miss Matilda Griffin!" and she flung out of the room, slamming the door, and leaving Miss Matilda to bust into tears, as was her reglar custom, and pour her loves and woas into the buzzom of Miss Kicksey.

CHAPTER IV

"HITTING THE NALE ON THE HEDD"

The nex morning, down came me and master to Lady Griffinses,—I amusing myself with the gals in the antyroom, he paying his devours to the ladies in the salong. Miss was thrumming on her gitter; my lady was before a great box of papers, busy with accounts, bankers' books, lawyers' letters, and what not. Law bless us! it's a kind of bisniss I should like well enuff; especially when my hannual account was seven or eight thousand on the right side, like my lady's. My lady in this house kep all these matters to herself. Miss was a vast deal too sentrimentle to mind business.

Miss Matilda's eyes sparkled as master came in; she pinted gracefully to a place on the sofy beside her, which Deuceace took. My lady only looked up for a moment, smiled very kindly, and down went her head among the papers agen, as busy as a B.

"Lady Griffin has had letters from London," says Miss, "from nasty lawyers and people. Come here and sit by me, you naughty man you!"

And down sat master. "Willingly," says he, "my dear Miss Griffin; why, I declare, it is quits a tete-a-tete."

"Well," says Miss (after the prillimnary flumries, in coarse), "we met a friend of yours at the embassy, Mr. Deuceace."

"My father, doubtless; he is a great friend of the ambassador, and surprised me myself by a visit the night before last."

"What a dear delightful old man! how he loves you, Mr. Deuceace!"

"Oh, amazingly!" says master, throwing his i's to heaven.

"He spoke of nothing but you, and such praises of you!"

Master breathed more freely. "He is very good, my dear father; but blind, as all fathers are, he is so partial and attached to me."

"He spoke of you being his favorite child, and regretted that you were not his eldest son. 'I can but leave him the small portion of a younger brother,' he said; 'but never mind, he has talents, a noble name, and an independence of his own.'"

"An independence? yes, oh yes; I am quite independent of my father."

"Two thousand pounds a year left you by your godmother; the very same you told us you know."

"Neither more nor less," says master, bobbing his head; "a sufficiency, my dear Miss Griffin,—to a man of my moderate habits an ample provision."

"By-the-by," cries out Lady Griffin, interrupting the conversation, "you who are talking about money matters there, I wish you would come to the aid of poor ME! Come, naughty boy, and help me out with this long long sum."

DIDN'T HE GO—that's all! My i, how his i's shone, as he skipt across the room, and seated himself by my lady!

"Look!" said she, "my agents write me over that they have received a remittance of 7,200 rupees, at 2s. 9d. a rupee. Do tell me what the sum is, in pounds and shillings;" which master did with great gravity.

"Nine hundred and ninety pounds. Good; I daresay you are right. I'm sure I can't go through the fatigue to see. And now comes another question. Whose money is this, mine or Matilda's? You see it is the interest of a sum in India, which we have not had occasion to touch; and, according to the terms of poor Sir George's will, I really don't know how to dispose of the money except to spend it. Matilda, what shall we do with it?"

"La, ma'am, I wish you would arrange the business yourself."

"Well, then, Algernon, YOU tell me;" and she laid her hand on his and looked him most pathetickly in the face.

"Why," says he, "I don't know how Sir George left his money; you must let me see his will, first."

"Oh, willingly."

Master's chair seemed suddenly to have got springs in the cushns; he was obliged to HOLD HIMSELF DOWN.

"Look here, I have only a copy, taken by my hand from Sir George's own manuscript. Soldiers, you know, do not employ lawyers much, and this was written on the night before going into action." And she read, "'I, George Griffin,' &c. &c.—you know how these things begin—'being now of sane mind'—um, um, um,—'leave to my friends, Thomas Abraham Hicks, a colonel in the H. E. I. Company's Service, and to John Monro Mackirkincroft (of the house of Huffle, Mackirkincroft, and Dobbs, at Calcutta), the whole of my property, to be realized as speedily as they may (consistently with the interests of the property), in trust for my wife, Leonora Emilia Griffin (born L. E. Kicksey), and my only legitimate child, Matilda Griffin. The interest resulting from such property to be paid to them, share and share alike; the principal to remain untouched, in the names of the said T. A. Hicks and J. M. Mackirkincroft, until the death of my wife, Leonora Emilia Griffin, when it shall be paid to my daughter, Matilda Griffin, her heirs, executors, or assigns.'"

"There," said my lady, "we won't read any more; all the rest is stuff. But now you know the whole business, tell us what is to be done with the money?"

"Why, the money, unquestionably, should be divided between you."

"Tant mieux, say I; I really thought it had been all Matilda's."

There was a paws for a minit or two after the will had been read. Master left the desk at which he had been seated with her ladyship, paced up and down the room for a while, and then came round to the place where Miss Matilda was seated. At last he said, in a low, trembling voice,—

"I am almost sorry, my dear Lady Griffin, that you have read that will to me; for an attachment such as mine must seem, I fear, mercenary, when the object of it is so greatly favored by worldly fortune. Miss Griffin—Matilda! I know I may say the word; your dear eyes grant me the permission. I need not tell you, or you, dear mother-in-law, how long, how fondly, I have adored you. My tender, my beautiful Matilda, I will not affect to say I have not read your heart ere this, and that I have not known the preference with which you have honored me. SPEAK IT, dear girl! from your own sweet lips: in the presence of an affectionate parent, utter the sentence which is to seal my happiness for life. Matilda, dearest Matilda! say, oh say, that you love me!"

Miss M. shivered, turned pail, rowled her eyes about, and fell on master's neck, whispering hodibly, "I DO!"

My lady looked at the pair for a moment with her teeth grinding, her i's glaring, her busm throbbing, and her face chock white; for all the world like Madam Pasty, in the oppra of "Mydear" (when she's goin to mudder her childring, you recklect); and out she flounced from the room, without a word, knocking down poar me, who happened to be very near the dor, and leaving my master along with his crook-back mistress.

I've repotted the speech he made to her pretty well. The fact is, I got it in a ruff copy; only on the copy it's wrote, "Lady Griffin, Leonora!" instead of "Miss Griffin, Matilda," as in the abuff, and so on.

Master had hit the right nail on the head this time, he thought: but his adventors an't over yet.

CHAPTER V

THE GRIFFIN'S CLAWS

Well, master had hit the right nail on the head this time: thanx to luck—the crooked one, to be sure, but then it had the GOOLD NOBB, which was the part Deuceace most valued, as well he should; being a connyshure as to the relletiff valyou of pretious metals, and much preferring virging goold like this to poor old battered iron like my Lady Griffin.

And so, in spite of his father (at which old noblemin Mr. Deuceace now snapt his fingers), in spite of his detts (which, to do him Justas, had never stood much in his way), and in spite of his povatty, idleness, extravagans, swindling, and debotcheries of all kinds (which an't GENERALLY very favorable to a young man who has to make his way in the world); in spite of all, there he was, I say, at the topp of the trea, the fewcher master of a perfect fortun, the defianced husband of a fool of a wife. What can mortial man want more? Vishns of ambishn now occupied his soal. Shooting boxes, oppra boxes, money boxes always full; hunters at Melton; a seat in the house of Commins: heaven knows what! and not a poar footman, who only describes what he's seen, and can't, in cors, pennytrate into the idears and the busms of men.

You may be shore that the three-cornered noats came pretty thick now from the Griffinses. Miss was always a-writing them befoar; and now, nite, noon, and mornink, breakfast, dinner, and sopper, in they came, till my pantry (for master never read 'em, and I carried 'em out) was puffickly intolrabble from the odor of musk, ambygrease, bargymot, and other sense with which they were impregniated. Here's the contense of three on 'em, which I've kep in my dex these twenty years as skeewriosities. Faw! I can smel 'em at this very minit, as I am copying them down.

BILLY DOO. No. I.

"Monday morning, 2 o'clock.

"'Tis the witching hour of night. Luna illumines my chamber, and falls upon my sleepless pillow. By her light I am inditing these words to thee, my Algernon. My brave and beautiful, my soul's lord! when shall the time come when the tedious night shall not separate us, nor the blessed day? Twelve! one! two! I have heard the bells chime, and the quarters, and never cease to think of my husband. My adored Percy, pardon the girlish confession,—I have kissed the letter at this place. Will thy lips press it too, and remain for a moment on the spot which has been equally saluted by your

"MATILDA?"

This was the FUST letter, and was brot to our house by one of the poar footmin, Fitzclarence, at sicks o'clock in the morning. I thot it was for life and death, and woak master at that extraorny hour, and gave it to him. I shall never forgit him, when he red it; he cramped it up, and he cust and swoar, applying to the lady who roat, the genlmn that brought it, and me who introjuiced it to his notice such a collection of epitafs as I seldum hered, excep at Billinxgit. The fact is thiss; for a fust letter, miss's noat was RATHER too strong and sentymentle. But that was her way; she was always reading melancholy stoary books—"Thaduse of Wawsaw," the "Sorrows of MacWhirter," and such like.

After about 6 of them, master never youzed to read them, but handid them over to me, to see if there was anythink in them which must be answered, in order to kip up appearuntses. The next letter is

No. II.

"BELOVED! to what strange madnesses will passion lead one! Lady Griffin, since your avowal yesterday, has not spoken a word to your poor Matilda; has declared that she will admit no one (heigho! not even you, my Algernon); and has locked herself in her own dressing-room. I do believe that she is JEALOUS, and fancies that you were in love with HER! Ha, ha! I could have told her ANOTHER TALE—n'est-ce pas? Adieu, adieu, adieu! A thousand thousand million kisses!

"M. G.

"Monday afternoon, 2 o'clock."

There was another letter kem before bedtime; for though me and master called at the Griffinses, we wairnt aloud to enter at no price. Mortimer and Fitzclarence grin'd at me, as much as to say we were going to be relations; but I don't spose master was very sorry when he was obleached to come back without seeing the fare objict of his affeckshns.

Well, on Chewsdy there was the same game; ditto on Wensday; only, when we called there, who should we see but our father, Lord Crabs, who was waiving his hand to Miss Kicksey, and saying HE SHOULD BE BACK TO DINNER AT 7, just as me and master came up the stares. There was no admittns for us though. "Bah! bah! never mind," says my lord, taking his son affeckshnately by the hand. "What, two strings to your bow; ay, Algernon? The dowager a little jealous, miss a little lovesick. But my lady's fit of anger will vanish, and I promise you, my boy, that you shall see your fair one to-morrow."

And so saying, my lord walked master down stares, looking at him as tender and affeckshnat, and speaking to him as sweet as posbill. Master did not know what to think of it. He never new what game his old father was at; only he somehow felt that he had got his head in a net, in spite of his suxess on Sunday. I knew it—I knew it quite well, as soon as I saw the old genlmn igsammin him by a kind of smile which came over his old face, and was somethink betwigst the angellic and the direbollicle.

But master's dowts were cleared up nex day and every thing was bright again. At brexfast, in comes a note with inclosier, boath of witch I here copy:—

No. IX.

"Thursday morning.

"Victoria, Victoria! Mamma has yielded at last; not her consent to our union, but her consent to receive you as before; and has promised to forget the past. Silly woman, how could she ever think of you as anything but the lover of your Matilda? I am in a whirl of delicious joy and passionate excitement. I have been awake all this long night, thinking of thee, my Algernon, and longing for the blissful hour of meeting.

"Come! M. G."

This is the inclosier from my lady:—

"I will not tell you that your behavior on Sunday did not deeply shock me. I had been foolish enough to think of other plans, and to fancy your heart (if you had any) was fixed elsewhere than on one at whose foibles you have often laughed with me, and whose person at least cannot have charmed you.

"My step-daughter will not, I presume, marry without at least going through the ceremony of asking my consent; I cannot, as yet, give it. Have I not reason to doubt whether she will be happy in trusting herself to you?

"But she is of age, and has the right to receive in her own house all those who may be agreeable to her,—certainly you, who are likely to be one day so nearly connected with her. If I have honest reason to believe that your love for Miss Griffin is sincere; if I find in a few months that you yourself are still desirous to marry her, I can, of course, place no further obstacles in your way.

"You are welcome, then, to return to our hotel. I cannot promise to receive you as I did of old; you would despise me if I did. I can promise, however, to think no more of all that has passed between us, and yield up my own happiness for that of the daughter of my dear husband.

"L. E. G."

Well, now, an't this a manly, straitforard letter enough, and natral from a woman whom we had, to confess the truth, treated most scuvvily? Master thought so, and went and made a tender, respeckful speach to Lady Griffin (a little flumry costs nothink). Grave and sorroflle he kist her hand, and, speakin in a very low adgitayted voice, calld Hevn to witness how he deplord that his conduct should ever have given rise to such an unfornt ideer; but if he might offer her esteem, respect, the warmest and tenderest admiration, he trusted she would accept the same, and a deal moar flumry of the kind, with dark, sollum glansis of the eyes, and plenty of white pockit-hankercher.

He thought he'd make all safe. Poar fool! he was in a net—sich a net as I never yet see set to ketch a roag in.

CHAPTER VI

THE JEWEL

The Shevalier de l'Orge, the young Frenchmin whom I wrote of in my last, who had been rather shy of his visits while master was coming it so very strong, now came back to his old place by the side of Lady Griffin: there was no love now, though, betwigst him and master, although the shevallier had got his lady back agin; Deuceace being compleatly devoted to his crookid Veanus.

The shevalier was a little, pale, moddist, insinifishnt creature; and I shoodn't have thought, from his appearants, would have the heart to do harm to a fli, much less to stand befor such a tremendious tiger and fire-eater as my master. But I see putty well, after a week, from his manner of going on—of speakin at master, and lookin at him, and olding his lips tight when Deuceace came into the room, and glaring at him with his i's, that he hated the Honrabble Algernon Percy.

Shall I tell you why? Because my Lady Griffin hated him: hated him wuss than pison, or the devvle, or even wuss than her daughter-in-law. Praps you phansy that the letter you have juss red was honest; praps you amadgin that the sean of the reading of the will came on by mere chans, and in the reglar cors of suckmstansies: it was all a GAME, I tell you—a reglar trap; and that extrodnar clever young man, my master, as neatly put his foot into it, as ever a pocher did in fesnt preserve.

The shevalier had his q from Lady Griffin. When Deuceace went off the feald, back came De l'Orge to her feet, not a witt less tender than befor. Por fellow, por fellow! he really loved this woman. He might as well have foln in love with a bore-constructor! He was so blinded and beat by the power wich she had got over him, that if she told him black was white he'd beleave it, or if she ordered him to commit murder, he'd do it: she wanted something very like it, I can tell you.

I've already said how, in the fust part of their acquaintance, master used to laff at De l'Orge's bad Inglish, and funny ways. The little creature had a thowsnd of these; and being small, and a Frenchman, master, in cors, looked on him with that good-humored kind of contemp which a good Brittn ot always to show. He rayther treated him like an intelligent munky than a man, and ordered him about as if he'd bean my lady's footman.

All this munseer took in very good part, until after the quarl betwigst master and Lady Griffin; when that lady took care to turn the tables. Whenever master and miss were not present (as I've heard the servants say), she used to laff at shevalliay for his obeajance and sivillatty to master. For her part, she wondered how a man of his birth could act a servnt: how any man could submit to such contemsheous behavior from another; and then she told him how Deuceace was always snearing at him behind his back; how, in fact, he ought to hate him corjaly, and how it was suttaly time to show his sperrit.

Well, the poar little man beleaved all this from his hart, and was angry or pleased, gentle or quarlsum, igsactly as my lady liked. There got to be frequint rows betwigst him and master; sharp words flung at each other across the dinner-table; dispewts about handing ladies their smeling-botls, or seeing them to their carridge; or going in and out of a roam fust, or any such nonsince.

"For hevn's sake," I heerd my lady, in the midl of one of these tiffs, say, pail, and the tears trembling in her i's, "do, do be calm, Mr. Deuceace. Monsieur de l'Orge, I beseech you to forgive him. You are, both of you, so esteemed, lov'd, by members of this family, that for its peace as well as your own, you should forbear to quarrel."

It was on the way to the Sally Mangy that this brangling had begun, and it ended jest as they were seating themselves. I shall never forgit poar little De l'Orge's eyes, when my lady said "both of you." He stair'd at my lady for a momint, turned pail, red, look'd wild, and then, going round to master, shook his hand as if he would have wrung it off. Mr. Deuceace only bow'd and grin'd, and turned away quite stately; Miss heaved a loud O from her busm, and looked up in his face with an igspreshn jest as if she could have eat him up with love; and the little shevalliay sate down to his soop-plate, and wus so happy, that I'm blest if he wasn't crying! He thought the widdow had made her declyration, and would have him; and so thought Deuceace, who look'd at her for some time mighty bitter and contempshus, and then fell a-talking with Miss.

Now, though master didn't choose to marry Lady Griffin, as he might have done, he yet thought fit to be very angry at the notion of her marrying anybody else; and so, consquintly, was in a fewry at this confision which she had made regarding her parshaleaty for the French shevaleer.

And this I've perseaved in the cors of my expearants through life, that when you vex him, a roag's no longer a roag: you find him out at onst when he's in a passion, for he shows, as it ware, his cloven foot the very instnt you tread on it. At least, this is what YOUNG roags do; it requires very cool blood and long practis to get over this pint, and not to show your pashn when you feel it and snarl when you are angry. Old Crabs wouldn't do it; being like another noblemin, of whom I heard the Duke of Wellington say, while waiting behind his graci's chair, that if you were kicking him from behind, no one standing before him would know it, from the bewtifle smiling igspreshn of his face. Young master hadn't got so far in the thief's grammer, and, when he was angry, show'd it. And it's also to be remarked (a very profownd observatin for a footmin, but we have i's though we DO wear plush britchis), it's to be remarked, I say, that one of these chaps is much sooner maid angry than another, because honest men yield to other people, roags never do; honest men love other people, roags only themselves; and the slightest thing which comes in the way of thir beloved objects sets them fewrious. Master hadn't led a life of gambling, swindling, and every kind of debotch to be good-tempered at the end of it, I prommis you.

He was in a pashun, and when he WAS in a pashn, a more insalent, insuffrable, overbearing broot didn't live.

This was the very pint to which my lady wished to bring him; for I must tell you, that though she had been trying all her might to set master and the shevalliay by the years, she had suxeaded only so far as to make them hate each profowndly: but somehow or other, the 2 cox wouldn't FIGHT.

I doan't think Deuceace ever suspected any game on the part of her ladyship, for she carried it on so admirally, that the quarls which daily took place betwigst him and the Frenchman never seemed to come from her; on the contry, she acted as the reglar pease-maker between them, as I've just shown in the tiff which took place at the door of the Sally Mangy. Besides, the 2 young men, though reddy enough to snarl, were natrally unwilling to come to bloes. I'll tell you why: being friends, and idle, they spent their mornins as young fashnabbles genrally do, at billiads, fensing, riding, pistle-shooting, or some such improoving study. In billiads, master beat the Frenchman hollow (and had won a pretious sight of money from him: but that's neither here nor there, or, as the French say, ontry noo); at pistle-shooting, master could knock down eight immidges out of ten, and De l'Orge seven; and in fensing, the Frenchman could pink the Honorable Algernon down evry one of his weskit buttns. They'd each of them been out more than onst, for every Frenchman will fight, and master had been obleag'd to do so in the cors of his bisniss; and knowing each other's curridg, as well as the fact that either could put a hundrid bolls running into a hat at 30 yards, they wairnt very willing to try such exparrymence upon their own hats with their own heads in them. So you see they kep quiet, and only grould at each other.

But to-day Deuceace was in one of his thundering black humers; and when in this way he wouldn't stop for man or devvle. I said that he walked away from the shevalliay, who had given him his hand in his sudden bust of joyfle good-humor; and who, I do bleave, would have hugd a she-bear, so very happy was he. Master walked away from him pale and hotty, and, taking his seat at table, no moor mindid the brandishments of Miss Griffin, but only replied to them with a pshaw, or a dam at one of us servnts, or abuse of the soop, or the wine; cussing and swearing like a trooper, and not like a well-bred son of a noble British peer.

"Will your ladyship," says he, slivering off the wing of a pully ally bashymall, "allow me to help you?"

"I thank you! no; but I will trouble Monsieur de l'Orge." And towards that gnlmn she turned, with a most tender and fasnating smile.

"Your ladyship has taken a very sudden admiration for Mr. de l'Orge's carving. You used to like mine once."

"You are very skilful; but to-day, if you will allow me, I will partake of something a little simpler."

The Frenchman helped; and, being so happy, in cors, spilt the gravy. A great blob of brown sos spurted on to master's chick, and myandrewed down his shert-collar and virging-white weskit.

"Confound you!" says he, "M. de l'Orge, you have done this on purpose." And down went his knife and fork, over went his tumbler of wine, a deal of it into poar Miss Griffinses lap, who looked fritened and ready to cry.

My lady bust into a fit of laffin, peel upon peel, as if it was the best joak in the world. De l'Orge giggled and grin'd too. "Pardong," says he; "meal pardong, mong share munseer." * And he looked as if he would have done it again for a penny.

* In the long dialogues, we have generally ventured to change the peculiar spelling of our friend Mr. Yellowplush.

The little Frenchman was quite in extasis; he found himself all of a suddn at the very top of the trea; and the laff for onst turned against his rivle: he actialy had the ordassaty to propose to my lady in English to take a glass of wine.

"Veal you," says he, in his jargin, "take a glas of Madere viz me, mi ladi?" And he looked round, as if he'd igsackly hit the English manner and pronunciation.

"With the greatest pleasure," says Lady G., most graciously nodding at him, and gazing at him as she drank up the wine. She'd refused master before, and THIS didn't increase his good-humer.

Well, they went on, master snarling, snapping, and swearing, making himself, I must confess, as much of a blaggard as any I ever see; and my lady employing her time betwigst him and the shevalliay, doing every think to irritate master, and flatter the Frenchmn. Desert came: and by this time, Miss was stock-still with fright, the chevaleer half tipsy with pleasure and gratafied vannaty, my lady puffickly raygent with smiles and master bloo with rage.

"Mr. Deuceace," says my lady, in a most winning voice, after a little chaffing (in which she only worked him up moar and moar), "may I trouble you for a few of those grapes? they look delicious."

For answer, master seas'd hold of the grayp dish, and sent it sliding down the table to De l'Orge; upsetting, in his way, fruit-plates, glasses, dickanters, and heaven knows what.

"Monsieur de l'Orge," says he, shouting out at the top of his voice, "have the goodness to help Lady Griffin. She wanted MY grapes long ago, and has found out they are sour!"

There was a dead paws of a moment or so.

"Ah!" says my lady, "vous osez m'insulter, devant mes gens, dans ma propre maison—c'est par trop fort, monsieur." And up she got, and flung out of the room. Miss followed her, screeching out, "Mamma—for God's sake—Lady Griffin!" and here the door slammed on the pair.

Her ladyship did very well to speak French. DE L'ORGE WOULD NOT HAVE UNDERSTOOD HER ELSE; as it was he heard quite enough; and as the door clikt too, in the presents of me, and Messeers Mortimer and Fitzclarence, the family footmen, he walks round to my master, and hits him a slap on the face, and says, "prends ca, menteur et lache!" which means, "Take that, you liar and coward!"—rayther strong igspreshns for one genlmn to use to another.

Master staggered back and looked bewildered; and then he gave a kind of a scream, and then he made a run at the Frenchman, and then me and Mortimer flung ourselves upon him, whilst Fitzclarence embraced the shevalliay.

"A demain!" says he, clinching his little fist, and walking away, not very sorry to git off.

When he was fairly down stares, we let go of master: who swallowed a goblit of water, and then pawsing a little and pullout his pus, he presented to Messeers Mortimer and Fitzclarence a luydor each. "I will give you five more to-morrow," says he, "if you will promise to keep this secrit."

And then he walked in to the ladies. "If you knew," says he, going up to Lady Griffin, and speaking very slow (in cors we were all at the keyhole), "the pain I have endured in the last minute, in consequence of the rudeness and insolence of which I have been guilty to your ladyship, you would think my own remorse was punishment sufficient, and would grant me pardon."

My lady bowed, and said she didn't wish for explanations. Mr. Deuceace was her daughter's guest, and not hers; but she certainly would never demean herself by sitting again at table with him. And so saying out she boltid again.

"Oh! Algernon! Algernon!" says Miss, in teers, "what is this dreadful mystery—these fearful shocking quarrels? Tell me, has anything happened? Where, where is the chevalier?"

Master smiled and said, "Be under no alarm, my sweetest Matilda. De l'Orge did not understand a word of the dispute; he was too much in love for that. He is but gone away for half an hour, I believe; and will return to coffee."

I knew what master's game was, for if miss had got a hinkling of the quarrel betwigst him and the Frenchman, we should have had her screeming at the "Hotel Mirabeu," and the juice and all to pay. He only stopt for a few minnits and cumfitted her, and then drove off to his friend, Captain Bullseye, of the Rifles; with whom, I spose, he talked over this unplesnt bisniss. We fownd, at our hotel, a note from De l'Orge, saying where his secknd was to be seen.

Two mornings after there was a parrowgraf in Gallynanny's Messinger, which I hear beg leaf to transcribe:—

"FEARFUL DUEL.—Yesterday morning, at six o'clock, a meeting took place, in the Bois de Boulogne, between the Hon. A. P. D—ce-ce, a younger son of the Earl of Cr-bs, and the Chevalier de l'O—. The chevalier was attended by Major de M—, of the Royal Guard, and the Hon. Mr. D— by Captain B-lls-ye, of the British Rifle Corps. As far as we have been able to learn the particulars of this deplorable affair, the dispute originated in the house of a lovely lady (one of the most brilliant ornaments of our embassy), and the duel took place on the morning ensuing.

"The chevalier (the challenged party, and the most accomplished amateur swordsman in Paris) waived his right of choosing the weapons, and the combat took place with pistols.

"The combatants were placed at forty paces, with directions to advance to a barrier which separated them only eight paces. Each was furnished with two pistols. Monsieur de l'O— fired almost immediately, and the ball took effect in the left wrist of his antagonist, who dropped the pistol which he held in that hand. He fired, however, directly with his right, and the chevalier fell to the ground, we fear mortally wounded. A ball has entered above his hip-joint, and there is very little hope that he can recover.

"We have heard that the cause of this desperate duel was a blow which the chevalier ventured to give to the Hon. Mr. D. If so, there is some reason for the unusual and determined manner in which the duel was fought.

"Mr. Deu—a-e returned to his hotel; whither his excellent father, the Right Hon. Earl of Cr-bs, immediately hastened on hearing of the sad news, and is now bestowing on his son the most affectionate parental attention. The news only reached his lordship yesterday at noon, while at breakfast with his Excellency Lord Bobtail, our ambassador. The noble earl fainted on receiving the intelligence; but in spite of the shock to his own nerves and health, persisted in passing last night by the couch of his son."

And so he did. "This is a sad business, Charles," says my lord to me, after seeing his son, and settling himself down in our salong. "Have you any segars in the house? And hark ye, send me up a bottle of wine and some luncheon. I can certainly not leave the neighborhood of my dear boy."

CHAPTER VII

THE CONSQUINSIES

The shevalliay did not die, for the ball came out of its own accord, in the midst of a violent fever and inflamayshn which was brot on by the wound. He was kept in bed for 6 weeks though, and did not recover for a long time after.

As for master, his lot, I'm sorry to say, was wuss than that of his advisary. Inflammation came on too; and, to make an ugly story short, they were obliged to take off his hand at the rist.

He bore it, in cors, like a Trojin, and in a month he too was well, and his wound heel'd; but I never see a man look so like a devvle as he used sometimes, when he looked down at the stump!

To be sure, in Miss Griffinses eyes, this only indeerd him the mor. She sent twenty noats a day to ask for him, calling him her beloved, her unfortunat, her hero, her wictim, and I dono what. I've kep some of the noats, as I tell you, and curiously sentimentle they are, beating the sorrows of MacWhirter all to nothing.

Old Crabs used to come offen, and consumed a power of wine and seagars at our house. I bleave he was at Paris because there was an exycution in his own house in England; and his son was a sure find (as they say) during his illness, and couldn't deny himself to the old genlmn. His eveninx my lord spent reglar at Lady Griffin's; where, as master was ill, I didn't go any more now, and where the shevalier wasn't there to disturb him.

"You see how that woman hates you, Deuceace," says my lord, one day, in a fit of cander, after they had been talking about Lady Griffin: "SHE HAS NOT DONE WITH YOU YET, I tell you fairly."

"Curse her," says master, in a fury, lifting up his maim'd arm—"curse her! but I will be even with her one day. I am sure of Matilda: I took care to put that beyond the reach of a failure. The girl must marry me, for her own sake."

"FOR HER OWN SAKE! O ho! Good, good!" My lord lifted his i's, and said gravely, "I understand, my dear boy: it is an excellent plan."

"Well," says master, grinning fearcely and knowingly at his exlent old father, "as the girl is safe, what harm can I fear from the fiend of a step-mother?"

My lord only gev a long whizzle, and, soon after, taking up his hat, walked off. I saw him sawnter down the Plas Vandome, and go in quite calmly to the old door of Lady Griffinses hotel. Bless his old face! such a puffickly good-natured, kind-hearted, merry, selfish old scoundrel, I never shall see again.

His lordship was quite right in saying to master that "Lady Griffin hadn't done with him." No moar she had. But she never would have thought of the nex game she was going to play, IF SOMEBODY HADN'T PUT HER UP TO IT. Who did? If you red the above passidge, and saw how a venrabble old genlmn took his hat, and sauntered down the Plas Vandome (looking hard and kind at all the nussary-maids—buns they call them in France—in the way), I leave you to guess who was the author of the nex scheam: a woman, suttnly, never would have pitcht on it.

In the fuss payper which I wrote concerning Mr. Deuceace's adventers, and his kind behayvior to Messrs. Dawkins and Blewitt, I had the honor of laying before the public a skidewl of my master's detts, in witch was the following itim:

"Bills of xchange and I.O.U.'s, 4963L. 0s. 0d."

The I.O.U.se were trifling, say a thowsnd pound. The bills amountid to four thowsnd moar.

Now, the lor is in France, that if a genlmn gives these in England, and a French genlmn gits them in any way, he can pursew the Englishman who has drawn them, even though he should be in France. Master did not know this fact—laboring under a very common mistak, that, when onst out of England, he might wissle at all the debts he left behind him.

My Lady Griffin sent over to her slissators in London, who made arrangemints with the persons who possest the fine collection of ortografs on stampt paper which master had left behind him; and they were glad enuff to take any oppertunity of getting back their money.

One fine morning, as I was looking about in the court-yard of our hotel, talking to the servant-gals, as was my reglar custom, in order to improve myself in the French languidge, one of them comes up to me and says, "Tenez, Monsieur Charles, down below in the office there is a bailiff, with a couple of gendarmes, who is asking for your master—a-t-il des dettes par hasard?"

I was struck all of a heap—the truth flasht on my mind's hi. "Toinette," says I, for that was the gal's name—"Toinette," says I, giving her a kiss, "keep them for two minits, as you valyou my affeckshn;" and then I gave her another kiss, and ran up stares to our chambers. Master had now pretty well recovered of his wound, and was aloud to drive abowt: it was lucky for him that he had the strength to move. "Sir, sir," says I, "the bailiffs are after you, and you must run for your life."

"Bailiff?" says he: "nonsense! I don't, thank heaven, owe a shilling to any man."

"Stuff, sir," says I, forgetting my respeck; "don't you owe money in England? I tell you the bailiffs are here, and will be on you in a moment."

As I spoke, cling cling, ling ling, goes the bell of the antyshamber, and there they were sure enough!

What was to be done? Quick as litening, I throws off my livry coat, claps my goold lace hat on master's head, and makes him put on my livry. Then I wraps myself up in his dressing-gown, and lolling down on the sofa, bids him open the dor.

There they were—the bailiff—two jondarms with him—Toinette, and an old waiter. When Toinette sees master, she smiles, and says: "Dis donc, Charles! ou est donc ton maitre? Chez lui, n'est-ce pas? C'est le jeune a monsieur," says she, curtsying to the bailiff.

The old waiter was just a-going to blurt out, "Mais ce n'est pas!" when Toinette stops him, and says, "Laissez donc passer ces messieurs, vieux bete;" and in they walk, the 2 jon d'arms taking their post in the hall.

Master throws open the salong doar very gravely, and touching MY hat says, "Have you any orders about the cab, sir?"

"Why, no, Chawls," says I; "I shan't drive out to-day."

The old bailiff grinned, for he understood English (having had plenty of English customers), and says in French, as master goes out, "I think, sir, you had better let your servant get a coach, for I am under the painful necessity of arresting you, au nom de la loi, for the sum of ninety-eight thousand seven hundred francs, owed by you to the Sieur Jacques Francois Lebrun, of Paris;" and he pulls out a number of bills, with master's acceptances on them sure enough.

"Take a chair, sir," says I; and down he sits; and I began to chaff him, as well as I could, about the weather, my illness, my sad axdent, having lost one of my hands, which was stuck into my busum, and so on.

At last, after a minnit or two, I could contane no longer, and bust out in a horse laff.

The old fellow turned quite pail, and began to suspect somethink. "Hola!" says he; "gendarmes! a moi! a moi! Je suis floue, vole," which means, in English, that he was reglar sold.

The jondarmes jumped into the room, and so did Toinette and the waiter. Grasefly rising from my arm-chare, I took my hand from my dressing-gownd, and, flinging it open, stuck up on the chair one of the neatest legs ever seen.

I then pinted majestickly—to what do you think?—to my PLUSH TITES! those sellabrated inigspressables which have rendered me famous in Yourope.

Taking the hint, the jondarmes and the servnts rord out laffing; and so did Charles Yellowplush, Esquire, I can tell you. Old Grippard the bailiff looked as if he would faint in his chare.

I heard a kab galloping like mad out of the hotel-gate, and knew then that my master was safe.

CHAPTER VIII

THE END OF MR. DEUCEACE'S HISTORY. LIMBO

My tail is droring rabidly to a close; my suvvice with Mr. Deuceace didn't continyou very long after the last chapter, in which I described my admiral strattyjam, and my singlar self-devocean. There's very few servnts, I can tell you, who'd have thought of such a contrivance, and very few moar would have eggsycuted it when thought of.

But, after all, beyond the trifling advantich to myself in selling master's roab de sham, which you, gentle reader, may remember I woar, and in dixcovering a fipun note in one of the pockets,—beyond this, I say, there was to poar master very little advantich in what had been done. It's true he had escaped. Very good. But Frans is not like Great Brittin; a man in a livry coat, with 1 arm, is pretty easily known, and caught, too, as I can tell you.

Such was the case with master. He coodn leave Paris, moarover, if he would. What was to become, in that case, of his bride—his unchbacked hairis? He knew that young lady's temprimong (as the Parishers say) too well to let her long out of his site. She had nine thousand a yer. She'd been in love a duzn times befor, and mite be agin. The Honrabble Algernon Deuceace was a little too wide awake to trust much to the constnsy of so very inflammable a young creacher. Heavn bless us, it was a marycle she wasn't earlier married! I do bleave (from suttn seans that past betwigst us) that she'd have married me, if she hadn't been sejuiced by the supearor rank and indianuity of the genlmn in whose survace I was.

Well, to use a commin igspreshn, the beaks were after him. How was he to manitch? He coodn get away from his debts, and he wooden quit the fare objict of his affeckshns. He was ableejd, then, as the French say, to lie perdew,—going out at night, like a howl out of a hivy-bush, and returning in the daytime to his roast. For its a maxum in France (and I wood it were followed in Ingland), that after dark no man is lible for his detts; and in any of the royal gardens—the Twillaries, the Pally Roil, or the Lucksimbug, for example—a man may wander from sunrise to evening, and hear nothing of the ojus dunns: they an't admitted into these places of public enjyment and rondyvoo any more than dogs; the centuries at the garden-gates having orders to shuit all such.

Master, then, was in this uncomfrable situation—neither liking to go nor to stay! peeping out at nights to have an interview with his miss; ableagd to shuffle off her repeated questions as to the reason of all this disgeise, and to talk of his two thowsnd a year jest as if he had it and didn't owe a shilling in the world.

Of course, now, he began to grow mighty eager for the marritch.

He roat as many noats as she had done befor; swoar against delay and cerymony; talked of the pleasures of Hyming, the ardship that the ardor of two arts should be allowed to igspire, the folly of waiting for the consent of Lady Griffin. She was but a step-mother, and an unkind one. Miss was (he said) a major, might marry whom she liked; and suttnly had paid Lady G. quite as much attention as she ought, by paying her the compliment to ask her at all.

And so they went on. The curious thing was, that when master was pressed about his cause for not coming out till night-time, he was misterus; and Miss Griffin, when asked why she wooden marry, igsprest, or rather, DIDN'T igspress, a simlar secrasy. Wasn't it hard? the cup seemed to be at the lip of both of 'em, and yet somehow, they could not manitch to take a drink.

But one morning, in reply to a most desprat epistol wrote by my master over night, Deuceace, delighted, gits an answer from his soal's beluffd, which ran thus:—

MISS GRIFFIN TO THE HON. A. P. DEUCEACE.

"DEAREST,—You say you would share a cottage with me; there is no need, luckily, for that! You plead the sad sinking of your spirits at our delayed union. Beloved, do you think MY heart rejoices at our separation? You bid me disregard the refusal of Lady Griffin, and tell me that I owe her no further duty.

"Adored Algernon! I can refuse you no more. I was willing not to lose a single chance of reconciliation with this unnatural step-mother. Respect for the memory of my sainted father bid me do all in my power to gain her consent to my union with you: nay, shall I own it? prudence dictated the measure; for to whom should she leave the share of money accorded to her by my father's will but to my father's child.

"But there are bounds beyond which no forbearance can go; and, thank heaven, we have no need of looking to Lady Griffin for sordid wealth: we have a competency without her. Is it not so, dearest Algernon?

"Be it as you wish, then, dearest, bravest, and best. Your poor Matilda has yielded to you her heart long ago; she has no longer need to keep back her name. Name the hour, and I will delay no more; but seek for refuge in your arms from the contumely and insult which meet me ever here.

"MATILDA.

"P.S. Oh, Algernon! if you did but know what a noble part your dear father has acted throughout, in doing his best endeavors to further our plans, and to soften Lady Griffin! It is not his fault that she is inexorable as she is. I send you a note sent by her to Lord Crabs; we will laugh at it soon, n'est-ce pas?"

II.

"MY LORD,—In reply to your demand for Miss Griffin's hand, in favor of your son, Mr. Algernon Deuceace, I can only repeat what I before have been under the necessity of stating to you,—that I do not believe a union with a person of Mr. Deuceace's character would conduce to my stepdaughter's happiness, and therefore REFUSE MY CONSENT. I will beg you to communicate the contents of this note to Mr. Deuceace; and implore you no more to touch upon a subject which you must be aware is deeply painful to me.

"I remain your lordship's most humble servant,

"L. E. GRIFFIN.

"THE RIGHT HON. THE EARL OF CRABS."

"Hang her ladyship!" says my master, "what care I for it?" As for the old lord who'd been so afishous in his kindness and advice, master recknsiled that pretty well, with thinking that his lordship knew he was going to marry ten thousand a year, and igspected to get some share of it; for he roat back the following letter to his father, as well as a flaming one to Miss:

"Thank you, my dear father, for your kindness in that awkward business. You know how painfully I am situated just now, and can pretty well guess BOTH THE CAUSES of my disquiet. A marriage with my beloved Matilda will make me the happiest of men. The dear girl consents, and laughs at the foolish pretensions of her mother-in-law. To tell you the truth, I wonder she yielded to them so long. Carry your kindness a step further, and find for us a parson, a license, and make us two into one. We are both major, you know; so that the ceremony of a guardian's consent is unnecessary.

"Your affectionate

"ALGERNON DEUCEACE.

"How I regret that difference between us some time back! Matters are changed now, and shall be more still AFTER THE MARRIAGE."

I knew what my master meant,—that he would give the old lord the money after he was married; and as it was probble that miss would see the letter he roat, he made it such as not to let her see two clearly into his present uncomfrable situation.

I took this letter along with the tender one for Miss, reading both of 'em, in course, by the way. Miss, on getting hers, gave an inegspressable look with the white of her i's, kist the letter, and prest it to her busm. Lord Crabs read his quite calm, and then they fell a-talking together; and told me to wait awhile, and I should git an anser.

After a deal of counseltation, my lord brought out a card, and there was simply written on it,

To-morrow, at the Ambassador's, at Twelve.

"Carry that back to your master, Chawls," says he, "and bid him not to fail."

You may be sure I stept back to him pretty quick, and gave him the card and the messinge. Master looked sattasfied with both; but suttnly not over happy; no man is the day before his marridge; much more his marridge with a hump-back, Harriss though she be.

Well, as he was a-going to depart this bachelor life, he did what every man in such suckmstances ought to do; he made his will,—that is, he made a dispasition of his property, and wrote letters to his creditors telling them of his lucky chance; and that after his marridge he would sutnly pay them every stiver. BEFORE, they must know his povvaty well enough to be sure that paymint was out of the question.

To do him justas, he seam'd to be inclined to do the thing that was right, now that it didn't put him to any inkinvenients to do so.

"Chawls," says he, handing me over a tenpun-note, "here's your wagis, and thank you for getting me out of the scrape with the bailiffs: when you are married, you shall be my valet out of liv'ry, and I'll treble your salary."

His vallit! praps his butler! Yes, thought I, here's a chance—a vallit to ten thousand a year. Nothing to do but to shave him, and read his notes, and let my whiskers grow; to dress in spick and span black, and a clean shut per day; muffings every night in the housekeeper's room; the pick of the gals in the servants' hall; a chap to clean my boots for me, and my master's opera bone reglar once a week. I knew what a vallit was as well as any genlmn in service; and this I can tell you, he's genrally a hapier, idler, handsomer, mor genlmnly man than his master. He has more money to spend, for genlmn WILL leave their silver in their waistcoat pockets; more suxess among the gals; as good dinners, and as good wine—that is, if he's friends with the butler: and friends in corse they will be if they know which way their interest lies.

But these are only cassels in the air, what the French call shutter d'Espang. It wasn't roat in the book of fate that I was to be Mr. Deuceace's vallit.

Days will pass at last—even days befor a wedding, (the longist and unpleasantist day in the whole of a man's life, I can tell you, excep, may be, the day before his hanging); and at length Aroarer dawned on the suspicious morning which was to unite in the bonds of Hyming the Honrable Algernon Percy Deuceace, Exquire, and Miss Matilda Griffin. My master's wardrobe wasn't so rich as it had been; for he'd left the whole of his nicknax and trumpry of dressing-cases and rob dy shams, his bewtifle museum of varnished boots, his curous colleckshn of Stulz and Staub coats, when he had been ableaged to quit so suddnly our pore dear lodginx at the Hotel Mirabew; and being incog at a friend's house, ad contentid himself with ordring a coople of shoots of cloves from a common tailor, with a suffishnt quantaty of linning.

Well, he put on the best of his coats—a blue; and I thought it my duty to ask him whether he'd want his frock again: he was good natured and said, "Take it and be hanged to you." Half-past eleven o'clock came, and I was sent to look out at the door, if there were any suspicious charicters (a precious good nose I have to find a bailiff out, I can tell you, and an i which will almost see one round a corner); and presenly a very modest green glass coach droave up, and in master stept. I didn't in corse, appear on the box; because, being known, my appearints might have compromised master. But I took a short cut, and walked as quick as posbil down to the Rue de Foburg St. Honore, where his exlnsy the English ambasdor lives, and where marridges are always performed betwigst English folk at Paris.

There is, almost nex door to the ambasdor's hotel, another hotel, of that lo kind which the French call cabbyrays, or wine-houses; and jest as master's green glass-coach pulled up, another coach drove off, out of which came two ladies, whom I knew pretty well,—suffiz, that one had a humpback, and the ingenious reader will know why SHE came there; the other was poor Miss Kicksey, who came to see her turned off.

Well, master's glass-coach droav up, jest as I got within a few yards of the door; our carridge, I say, droav up, and stopt. Down gits coachmin to open the door, and comes I to give Mr. Deuceace an arm, when out of the cabaray shoot four fellows, and draw up betwigst the coach and embassy-doar; two other chaps go to the other doar of the carridge, and, opening it, one says—"Rendez-vous, M. Deuceace! Je vous arrete au nom de la loi!" (which means, "Get out of that, Mr. D.; you are nabbed and no mistake.") Master turned gashly pail, and sprung to the other side of the coach, as if a serpint had stung him. He flung open the door, and was for making off that way; but he saw the four chaps standing betwigst libbarty and him. He slams down the front window, and screams out, "Fouettez, cocher!" (which means, "Go it, coachmm!") in a despert loud voice; but coachmin wooden go it, and besides was off his box.

The long and short of the matter was, that jest as I came up to the door two of the bums jumped into the carridge. I saw all; I knew my duty, and so very mornfly I got up behind.

"Tiens," says one of the chaps in the street; "c'est ce drole qui nous a floure l'autre jour." I knew 'em, but was too melumcolly to smile.

"Ou irons-nous donc?" says coachmin to the genlmn who had got inside.

A deep woice from the intearor shouted out, in reply to the coachmin, "A SAINTE PELAGIE!"

And now, praps, I ot to dixcribe to you the humors of the prizn of Sainte Pelagie, which is the French for Fleat, or Queen's Bentch: but on this subject I'm rather shy of writing, partly because the admiral Boz has, in the history of Mr. Pickwick, made such a dixcripshun of a prizn, that mine wooden read very amyousingly afterwids; and, also, because, to tell you the truth, I didn't stay long in it, being not in a humer to waist my igsistance by passing away the ears of my youth in such a dull place.

My fust errint now was, as you may phansy, to carry a noat from master to his destined bride. The poar thing was sadly taken aback, as I can tell you, when she found, after remaining two hours at the Embassy, that her husband didn't make his appearance. And so, after staying on and on, and yet seeing no husband, she was forsed at last to trudge dishconslit home, where I was already waiting for her with a letter from my master.

There was no use now denying the fact of his arrest, and so he confest it at onst: but he made a cock-and-bull story of treachery of a friend, infimous fodgery, and heaven knows what. However, it didn't matter much; if he had told her that he had been betrayed by the man in the moon, she would have bleavd him.

Lady Griffin never used to appear now at any of my visits. She kep one drawing-room, and Miss dined and lived alone in another; they quarld so much that praps it was best they should live apart; only my Lord Crabs used to see both, comforting each with that winning and innsnt way he had. He came in as Miss, in tears, was lisning to my account of master's seazure, and hoping that the prisn wasn't a horrid place, with a nasty horrid dunjeon, and a dreadfle jailer, and nasty horrid bread and water. Law bless us! she had borrod her ideers from the novvles she had been reading!

"O my lord, my lord," says she, "have you heard this fatal story?"

"Dearest Matilda, what? For heaven's sake, you alarm me! What—yes—no—is it—no, it can't be! Speak!" says my lord, seizing me by the choler of my coat. "What has happened to my boy?"

"Please you, my lord," says I, "he's at this moment in prisn, no wuss,—having been incarserated about two hours ago."

"In prison! Algernon in prison! 'tis impossible! Imprisoned, for what sum? Mention it, and I will pay to the utmost farthing in my power."

"I'm sure your lordship is very kind," says I (recklecting the sean betwixgst him and master, whom he wanted to diddil out of a thowsand lb.); "and you'll be happy to hear he's only in for a trifle. Five thousand pound is, I think, pretty near the mark."

"Five thousand pounds!—confusion!" says my lord, clasping his hands, and looking up to heaven, "and I have not five hundred! Dearest Matilda, how shall we help him?"

"Alas, my lord, I have but three guineas, and you know how Lady Griffin has the—"

"Yes, my sweet child, I know what you would say; but be of good cheer—Algernon, you know, has ample funds of his own."

Thinking my lord meant Dawkins's five thousand, of which, to be sure, a good lump was left, I held my tung; but I cooden help wondering at Lord Crabs's igstream compashn for his son, and Miss, with her 10,000L. a year, having only 3 guineas is her pockit.

I took home (bless us, what a home!) a long and very inflamble letter from Miss, in which she dixscribed her own sorror at the disappointment; swoar she lov'd him only the moar for his misfortns; made light of them; as a pusson for a paltry sum of five thousand pound ought never to be cast down, 'specially as he had a certain independence in view; and vowed that nothing, nothing, should ever injuice her to part from him, etsettler, etsettler.

I told master of the conversation which had past betwigst me and my lord, and of his handsome offers, and his horrow at hearing of his son's being taken; and likewise mentioned how strange it was that Miss should only have 3 guineas, and with such a fortn: bless us, I should have thot that she would always have carried a hundred thowsnd lb. in her pockit!

At this master only said Pshaw! But the rest of the story about his father seemed to dixquiet him a good deal, and he made me repeat it over agin.

He walked up and down the room agytated, and it seam'd as if a new lite was breaking in upon him.

"Chawls," says he, "did you observe—did Miss—did my father seem PARTICULARLY INTIMATE with Miss Griffin?"

"How do you mean, sir?" says I.

"Did Lord Crabs appear very fond of Miss Griffin?"

"He was suttnly very kind to her."

"Come, sir, speak at once: did Miss Griffin seem very fond of his lordship?"

"Why, to tell the truth, sir, I must say she seemed VERY fond of him."

"What did he call her?"

"He called her his dearest gal."

"Did he take her hand?"

"Yes, and he—"

"And he what?"

"He kist her, and told her not to be so wery down-hearted about the misfortn which had hapnd to you."

"I have it now!" says he, clinching his fist, and growing gashly pail—"I have it now—the infernal old hoary scoundrel! the wicked, unnatural wretch! He would take her from me!" And he poured out a volley of oaves which are impossbill to be repeatid here.

I thot as much long ago: and when my lord kem with his vizits so pretious affeckshnt at my Lady Griffinses, I expected some such game was in the wind. Indeed, I'd heard a somethink of it from the Griffinses servnts, that my lord was mighty tender with the ladies.

One thing, however, was evident to a man of his intleckshal capassaties; he must either marry the gal at onst, or he stood very small chance of having her. He must get out of limbo immediantly, or his respectid father might be stepping into his vaykint shoes. Oh! he saw it all now—the fust attempt at arest, the marridge fixt at 12 o'clock, and the bayliffs fixt to come and intarup the marridge!—the jewel, praps, betwigst him and De l'Orge: but no, it was the WOMAN who did that—a MAN don't deal such fowl blows, igspecially a father to his son: a woman may, poar thing!—she's no other means of reventch, and is used to fight with underhand wepns all her life through.

Well, whatever the pint might be, this Deuceace saw pretty clear that he'd been beat by his father at his own game—a trapp set for him onst, which had been defitted by my presnts of mind—another trap set afterwids, in which my lord had been suxesfle. Now, my lord, roag as he was, was much too good-natured to do an unkind ackshn, mearly for the sake of doing it. He'd got to that pich that he didn't mind injaries—they were all fair play to him—he gave 'em, and reseav'd them, without a thought of mallis. If he wanted to injer his son, it was to benefick himself. And how was this to be done? By getting the hairiss to himself, to be sure. The Honrabble Mr. D. didn't say so; but I knew his feelinx well enough—he regretted that he had not given the old genlmn the money he askt for.

Poar fello! he thought he had hit it; but he was wide of the mark after all.

Well, but what was to be done? It was clear that he must marry the gal at any rate—cootky coot, as the French say: that is, marry her, and hang the igspence.

To do so he must first git out of prisn—to get out of prisn he must pay his debts—and to pay his debts, he must give every shilling he was worth. Never mind: four thousand pound is a small stake to a reglar gambler, igspecially when he must play it, or rot for life in prisn; and when, if he plays it well, it will give him ten thousand a year.

So, seeing there was no help for it, he maid up his mind, and accordingly wrote the follying letter to Miss Griffin:—

"MY ADORED MATILDA,—Your letter has indeed been a comfort to a poor fellow, who had hoped that this night would have been the most blessed in his life, and now finds himself condemned to spend it within a prison wall! You know the accursed conspiracy which has brought these liabilities upon me, and the foolish friendship which has cost me so much. But what matters! We have, as you say, enough, even though I must pay this shameful demand upon me; and five thousand pounds are as nothing, compared to the happiness which I lose in being separated a night from thee! Courage, however! If I make a sacrifice it is for you; and I were heartless indeed if I allowed my own losses to balance for a moment against your happiness.

"Is it not so, beloved one? IS not your happiness bound up with mine, in a union with me? I am proud to think so—proud, too, to offer such a humble proof as this of the depth and purity of my affection.

"Tell me that you will still be mine; tell me that you will be mine tomorrow; and to-morrow these vile chains shall be removed, and I will be free once more—or if bound, only bound to you! My adorable Matilda! my betrothed bride! Write to me ere the evening closes, for I shall never be able to shut my eyes in slumber upon my prison couch, until they have been first blessed by the sight of a few words from thee! Write to me, love! write to me! I languish for the reply which is to make or mar me for ever. Your affectionate

"A. P. D."

Having polisht off this epistol, master intrustid it to me to carry, and bade me at the same time to try and give it into Miss Griffin's hand alone. I ran with it to Lady Griffinses. I found Miss, as I desired, in a sollatary condition; and I presented her with master's pafewmed Billy.

She read it, and the number of size to which she gave vint, and the tears which she shed, beggar digscription. She wep and sighed until I thought she would bust. She even claspt my hand in her's, and said, "O Charles! is he very, very miserable?"

"He is, ma'am," says I; "very miserable indeed—nobody, upon my honor, could be miserablerer."

On hearing this pethetic remark, her mind was made up at onst: and sitting down to her eskrewtaw, she immediantly ableaged master with an answer. Here it is in black and white:

"My prisoned bird shall pine no more, but fly home to its nest in these arms! Adored Algernon, I will meet thee to-morrow, at the same place, at the same hour. Then, then, it will be impossible for aught but death to divide us.

"M. G."

This kind of flumry style comes, you see, of reading novvles, and cultivating littery purshuits in a small way. How much better is it to be puffickly ignorant of the hart of writing, and to trust to the writing of the heart. This is MY style: artyfiz I despise, and trust compleatly to natur: but revnong a no mootong, as our continental friends remark: to that nice white sheep, Algernon Percy Deuceace, Exquire; that wenrabble old ram, my Lord Crabs his father; and that tender and dellygit young lamb, Miss Matilda Griffin.

She had just foalded up into its proper triangular shape the noat transcribed abuff, and I was just on the point of saying, according to my master's orders, "Miss, if you please, the Honrabble Mr. Deuceace would be very much ableaged to you to keep the seminary which is to take place to-morrow a profound se—," when my master's father entered, and I fell back to the door. Miss, without a word, rusht into his arms, burst into teers agin, as was her reglar way (it must be confest she was of a very mist constitution), and showing to him his son's note, cried, "Look, my dear lord, how nobly your Algernon, OUR Algernon, writes to me. Who can doubt, after this, of the purity of his matchless affection?"

My lord took the letter, read it, seamed a good deal amyoused, and returning it to its owner, said, very much to my surprise, "My dear Miss Griffin, he certainly does seem in earnest; and if you choose to make this match without the consent of your mother-in-law, you know the consequence, and are of course your own mistress."

"Consequences!—for shame, my lord! A little money, more or less, what matters it to two hearts like ours?"

"Hearts are very pretty things, my sweet young lady, but Three-per-Cents are better."

"Nay, have we not an ample income of our own, without the aid of Lady Griffin?"

My lord shrugged his shoulders. "Be it so, my love," says he. "I'm sure I can have no other reason to prevent a union which is founded upon such disinterested affection."

And here the conversation dropt. Miss retired, clasping her hands, and making play with the whites of her i's. My lord began trotting up and down the room, with his fat hands stuck in his britchis pockits, his countnince lighted up with igstream joy, and singing, to my inordnit igstonishment:

"See the conquering hero comes!
Tiddy diddy doll—tiddy doll, doll, doll."

He began singing this song, and tearing up and down the room like mad. I stood amazd—a new light broke in upon me. He wasn't going, then, to make love to Miss Griffin! Master might marry her! Had she not got the for—?

I say, I was just standing stock still, my eyes fixt, my hands puppindicklar, my mouf wide open and these igstrordinary thoughts passing in my mind, when my lord having got to the last "doll" of his song, just as I came to the sillible "for" of my ventriloquism, or inward speech—we had eatch jest reached the pint digscribed, when the meditations of both were sudnly stopt, by my lord, in the midst of his singin and trottin match, coming bolt up aginst poar me, sending me up against one end of the room, himself flying back to the other: and it was only after considrabble agitation that we were at length restored to anything like a liquilibrium.

"What, YOU here, you infernal rascal?" says my lord.

"Your lordship's very kind to notus me," says I; "I am here." And I gave him a look.

He saw I knew the whole game.

And after whisling a bit, as was his habit when puzzled (I bleave he'd have only whisled if he had been told he was to be hanged in five minits), after whisling a bit, he stops sudnly, and coming up to me, says:

"Hearkye, Charles, this marriage must take place to-morrow."

"Must it, sir?" says I; "now, for my part, I don't think—"

"Stop, my good fellow; if it does not take place, what do you gain?"

This stagger'd me. If it didn't take place, I only lost a situation, for master had but just enough money to pay his detts; and it wooden soot my book to serve him in prisn or starving.

"Well," says my lord, "you see the force of my argument. Now, look here!" and he lugs out a crisp, fluttering, snowy HUNDRED-PUN NOTE! "If my son and Miss Griffin are married to-morrow, you shall have this; and I will, moreover, take you into my service, and give you double your present wages."

Flesh and blood cooden bear it. "My lord," says I, laying my hand upon my busm, "only give me security, and I'm yours for ever."

The old noblemin grin'd, and pattid me on the shoulder. "Right, my lad," says he, "right—you're a nice promising youth. Here is the best security." And he pulls out his pockit-book, returns the hundred-pun bill, and takes out one for fifty. "Here is half to-day; to-morrow you shall have the remainder."

My fingers trembled a little as I took the pretty fluttering bit of paper, about five times as big as any sum of money I had ever had in my life. I cast my i upon the amount: it was a fifty sure enough—a bank poss-bill, made payable to Leonora Emilia Griffin, and indorsed by her. The cat was out of the bag. Now, gentle reader, I spose you begin to see the game.

"Recollect, from this day you are in my service."

"My lord, you overpoar me with your faviors."

"Go to the devil, sir," says he: "do your duty, and hold your tongue."

And thus I went from the service of the Honorabble Algernon Deuceace to that of his exlnsy the Right Honorabble Earl of Crabs.

On going back to prisn, I found Deuceace locked up in that oajus place to which his igstravygansies had deservedly led him; and felt for him, I must say, a great deal of contemp. A raskle such as he—a swindler, who had robbed poar Dawkins of the means of igsistance; who had cheated his fellow-roag, Mr. Richard Blewitt, and who was making a musnary marridge with a disgusting creacher like Miss Griffin, didn merit any compashn on my purt; and I determined quite to keep secret the suckmstansies of my privit interew with his exlnsy my presnt master.

I gev him Miss Griffinses trianglar, which he read with a satasfied air. Then, turning to me, says he: "You gave this to Miss Griffin alone?"

"Yes, sir."

"You gave her my message?"

"Yes, sir."

"And you are quite sure Lord Crabs was not there when you gave either the message or the note?"

"Not there upon my honor," says I.

"Hang your honor, sir! Brush my hat and coat, and go CALL A COACH—do you hear?"

I did as I was ordered; and on coming back found master in what's called, I think, the greffe of the prisn. The officer in waiting had out a great register, and was talking to master in the French tongue, in coarse; a number of poar prisners were looking eagerly on.

"Let us see, my lor," says he; "the debt is 98,700 francs; there are capture expenses, interest so much; and the whole sum amounts to a hundred thousand francs, moins 13."

Deuceace, in a very myjestic way, takes out of his pocketbook four thowsnd pun notes. "This is not French money, but I presume that you know it, M. Greffier," says he.

The greffier turned round to old Solomon, a money-changer, who had one or two clients in the prisn, and hapnd luckily to be there. "Les billets sont bons," says he. "Je les prendrai pour cent mille douze cent francs, et j'espere, my lor, de vous revoir."

"Good," says the greffier; "I know them to be good, and I will give my lor the difference, and make out his release."

Which was done. The poar debtors gave a feeble cheer, as the great dubble iron gates swung open and clang to again, and Deuceace stept out and me after him, to breathe the fresh hair.

He had been in the place but six hours, and was now free again—free, and to be married to ten thousand a year nex day. But, for all that, he lookt very faint and pale. He HAD put down his great stake; and when he came out of Sainte Pelagie, he had but fifty pounds left in the world!

Never mind—when onst the money's down, make your mind easy; and so Deuceace did. He drove back to the Hotel Mirabew, where he ordered apartmince infinately more splendid than befor; and I pretty soon told Toinette, and the rest of the suvvants, how nobly he behayved, and how he valyoud four thousnd pound no more than ditch water. And such was the consquincies of my praises, and the poplarity I got for us boath, that the delighted landlady immediantly charged him dubble what she would have done, if it hadn been for my stoaries.

He ordered splendid apartmince, then, for the nex week; a carridge-and-four for Fontainebleau to-morrow at 12 precisely; and having settled all these things, went quietly to the "Roshy de Cancale," where he dined: as well he might, for it was now eight o'clock. I didn't spare the shompang neither that night, I can tell you; for when I carried the note he gave me for Miss Griffin in the evening, informing her of his freedom, that young lady remarked my hagitated manner of walking and speaking, and said, "Honest Charles! he is flusht with the events of the day. Here, Charles, is a napoleon; take it and drink to your mistress."

I pockitid it; but, I must say, I didn't like the money—it went against my stomick to take it.

CHAPTER IX

THE MARRIAGE

Well, the nex day came: at 12 the carridge-and-four was waiting at the ambasdor's doar; and Miss Griffin and the faithfle Kicksey were punctial to the apintment.

I don't wish to digscribe the marridge seminary—how the embasy chapling jined the hands of this loving young couple—how one of the embasy footmin was called in to witness the marridge—how Miss wep and fainted as usial—and how Deuceace carried her, fainting, to the brisky, and drove off to Fontingblo, where they were to pass the fust weak of the honey-moon. They took no servnts, because they wisht, they said, to be privit. And so, when I had shut up the steps, and bid the postilion drive on, I bid ajew to the Honrabble Algernon, and went off strait to his exlent father.

"Is it all over, Chawls?" said he.

"I saw them turned off at igsactly a quarter past 12, my lord," says I.

"Did you give Miss Griffin the paper, as I told you, before her marriage?"

"I did, my lord, in the presents of Mr. Brown, Lord Bobtail's man; who can swear to her having had it."

I must tell you that my lord had made me read a paper which Lady Griffin had written, and which I was comishnd to give in the manner menshnd abuff. It ran to this effect:—

"According to the authority given me by the will of my late dear husband, I forbid the marriage of Miss Griffin with the Honorable Algernon Percy Deuceace. If Miss Griffin persists in the union, I warn her that she must abide by the consequences of her act.

"LEONORA EMILIA GRIFFIN."

"RUE DE RIVOLI, May 8, 1818."

When I gave this to Miss as she entered the cortyard, a minnit before my master's arrivle, she only read it contemptiously, and said, "I laugh at the threats of Lady Griffin;" and she toar the paper in two, and walked on, leaning on the arm of the faithful and obleaging Miss Kicksey.

I picked up the paper for fear of axdents, and brot it to my lord. Not that there was any necessaty; for he'd kep a copy, and made me and another witniss (my Lady Griffin's solissator) read them both, before he sent either away.

"Good!" says he; and he projuiced from his potfolio the fello of that bewchus fifty-pun note, which he'd given me yesterday. "I keep my promise, you see, Charles," says he. "You are now in Lady Griffin's service, in the place of Mr. Fitzclarence, who retires. Go to Froje's, and get a livery."

"But, my lord," says I, "I was not to go into Lady Griffnses service, according to the bargain, but into—"

"It's all the same thing," says he; and he walked off. I went to Mr. Froje's, and ordered a new livry; and found, likwise, that our coachmin and Munseer Mortimer had been there too. My lady's livery was changed, and was now of the same color as my old coat at Mr. Deuceace's; and I'm blest if there wasn't a tremenjious great earl's corronit on the butins, instid of the Griffin rampint, which was worn befoar.

I asked no questions, however, but had myself measured; and slep that night at the Plas Vandome. I didn't go out with the carridge for a day or two, though; my lady only taking one footmin, she said, until HER NEW CARRIDGE was turned out.

I think you can guess what's in the wind NOW!

I bot myself a dressing-case, a box of Ody colong, a few duzen lawn sherts and neckcloths, and other things which were necessary for a genlmn in my rank. Silk stockings was provided by the rules of the house. And I completed the bisniss by writing the follying ginteel letter to my late master:—

"CHARLES YELLOWPLUSH, ESQUIRE, TO THE HONORABLE A. P. DEUCEACE.

"SUR,—Suckmstansies have acurd sins I last had the honner of wating on you, which render it impossbil that I should remane any longer in your suvvice. I'll thank you to leave out my thinx, when they come home on Sattady from the wash.

"Your obeajnt servnt,

"CHARLES YELLOWPLUSH."

"PLAS VENDOME."

The athography of the abuv noat, I confess, is atrocious; but ke voolyvoo? I was only eighteen, and hadn then the expearance in writing which I've enjide sins.

Having thus done my jewty in evry way, I shall prosead, in the nex chapter, to say what hapnd in my new place.

CHAPTER X

THE HONEY-MOON

The weak at Fontingblow past quickly away; and at the end of it, our son and daughter-in-law—a pare of nice young tuttle-duvs—returned to their nest, at the Hotel Mirabew. I suspeck that the COCK turtle-dove was preshos sick of his barging.

When they arriv'd, the fust thing they found on their table was a large parsle wrapt up in silver paper, and a newspaper, and a couple of cards, tied up with a peace of white ribbing. In the parsle was a hansume piece of plum-cake, with a deal of sugar. On the cards was wrote, in Goffick characters,

Earl of Crabs.

And, in very small Italian,

Countess of Crabs.

And in the paper was the following parrowgraff:—

"MARRIAGE IN HIGH LIFE.—Yesterday, at the British embassy, the Right Honorable John Augustus Altamont Plantagenet, Earl of Crabs, to Leonora Emilia, widow of the late Lieutenant-General Sir George Griffin, K. C. B. An elegant dejeune was given to the happy couple by his Excellency Lord Bobtail, who gave away the bride. The elite of the foreign diplomacy, the Prince Talleyrand and Marshal the Duke of Dalmatia on behalf of H. M. the King of France, honored the banquet and the marriage ceremony. Lord and Lady Crabs intend passing a few weeks at Saint Cloud."

The above dockyments, along with my own triffling billy, of which I have also givn a copy, greated Mr. and Mrs. Deuceace on their arrivle from Fontingblo. Not being present, I can't say what Deuceace said; but I can fancy how he LOOKT, and how poor Mrs. Deuceace lookt. They weren't much inclined to rest after the fiteeg of the junny; for, in 1/2 an hour after their arrival at Paris, the hosses were put to the carridge agen, and down they came thundering to our country-house at St. Cloud (pronounst by those absud Frenchmin Sing Kloo), to interrup our chaste loves and delishs marridge injyments.

My lord was sittn in a crimson satan dressing-gown, lolling on a sofa at an open windy, smoking seagars, as ushle; her ladyship, who, to du her justice, didn mind the smell, occupied another end of the room, and was working, in wusted, a pare of slippers, or an umbrellore case, or a coal-skittle, or some such nonsints. You would have thought to have sean 'em that they had been married a sentry, at least. Well, I bust in upon this conjugal tator-tator, and said, very much alarmed, "My lord, here's your son and daughter-in-law."

"Well," says my lord, quite calm, "and what then?"

"Mr. Deuceace!" says my lady, starting up, and looking fritened.

"Yes, my love, my son; but you need not be alarmed. Pray, Charles, say that Lady Crabs and I will be very happy to see Mr. and Mrs. Deuceace; and that they must excuse us receiving them en famille. Sit still, my blessing—take things coolly. Have you got the box with the papers?"

My lady pointed to a great green box—the same from which she had taken the papers, when Deuceace fust saw them,—and handed over to my lord a fine gold key. I went out, met Deuceace and his wife on the stepps, gave my messinge, and bowed them palitely in.

My lord didn't rise, but smoaked away as usual (praps a little quicker, but I can't say); my lady sat upright, looking handsum and strong. Deuceace walked in, his left arm tied to his breast, his wife and hat on the other. He looked very pale and frightened; his wife, poar thing! had her head berried in her handkerchief, and sobd fit to break her heart.

Miss Kicksey, who was in the room (but I didn't mention her, she was less than nothink in our house), went up to Mrs. Deuceace at onst, and held out her arms—she had a heart, that old Kicksey, and I respect her for it. The poor hunchback flung herself into Miss's arms, with a kind of whooping screech, and kep there for some time, sobbing in quite a historical manner. I saw there was going to be a sean, and so, in cors, left the door ajar.

"Welcome to Saint Cloud, Algy my boy!" says my lord, in a loud, hearty voice. "You thought you would give us the slip, eh, you rogue? But we knew it, my dear fellow: we knew the whole affair—did we not, my soul?—and you see, kept our secret better than you did yours."

"I must confess, sir," says Deuceace, bowing, "that I had no idea of the happiness which awaited me in the shape of a mother-in-law."

"No, you dog; no, no," says my lord, giggling: "old birds, you know, not to be caught with chaff, like young ones. But here we are, all spliced and happy, at last. Sit down, Algernon; let us smoke a segar, and talk over the perils and adventures of the last month. My love," says my lord, turning to his lady, "you have no malice against poor Algernon, I trust? Pray shake HIS HAND." (A grin.)

But my lady rose and said, "I have told Mr. Deuceace, that I never wished to see him, or speak to him, more. I see no reason, now, to change my opinion." And herewith she sailed out of the room, by the door through which Kicksey had carried poor Mrs. Deuceace.

"Well, well," says my lord, as Lady Crabs swept by, "I was in hopes she had forgiven you; but I know the whole story, and I must confess you used her cruelly ill. Two strings to your bow!—that was your game, was it, you rogue?"

"Do you mean, my lord, that you know all that past between me and Lady Grif—Lady Crabs, before our quarrel?"

"Perfectly—you made love to her, and she was almost in love with you; you jilted her for money, she got a man to shoot your hand off in revenge: no more dice-boxes, now, Deuceace; no more sauter la coupe. I can't think how the deuce you will manage to live without them."

"Your lordship is very kind; but I have given up play altogether," says Deuceace, looking mighty black and uneasy.

"Oh, indeed! Benedick has turned a moral man, has he? This is better and better. Are you thinking of going into the church, Deuceace?"

"My lord, may I ask you to be a little more serious?"

"Serious! a quoi bon? I am serious—serious in my surprise that, when you might have had either of these women, you should have preferred that hideous wife of yours."

"May I ask you, in turn, how you came to be so little squeamish about a wife, as to choose a woman who had just been making love to your own son?" says Deuceace, growing fierce.

"How can you ask such a question? I owe forty thousand pounds—there is an execution at Sizes Hall—every acre I have is in the hands of my creditors; and that's why I married her. Do you think there was any love? Lady Crabs is a dev'lish fine woman, but she's not a fool—she married me for my coronet, and I married her for her money."

"Well, my lord, you need not ask me, I think, why I married the daughter-in-law."

"Yes, but I DO, my dear boy. How the deuce are you to live? Dawkins's five thousand pounds won't last forever; and afterwards?"

"You don't mean, my lord—you don't—I mean, you can't— D—!" says he, starting up, and losing all patience, "you don't dare to say that Miss Griffin had not a fortune of ten thousand a year?"

My lord was rolling up, and wetting betwigst his lips, another segar; he lookt up, after he had lighted it, and said quietly—

"Certainly, Miss Griffin had a fortune of ten thousand a year."

"Well, sir, and has she not got it now? Has she spent it in a week?"

"SHE HAS NOT GOT A SIX-PENCE NOW: SHE MARRIED WITHOUT HER MOTHER'S CONSENT!"

Deuceace sunk down in a chair; and I never see such a dreadful picture of despair as there was in the face of that retchid man!—he writhed, and nasht his teeth, he tore open his coat, and wriggled madly the stump of his left hand, until, fairly beat, he threw it over his livid pale face, and sinking backwards, fairly wept alowd.

Bah! it's a dreddfle thing to hear a man crying! his pashn torn up from the very roots of his heart, as it must be before it can git such a vent. My lord, meanwhile, rolled his segar, lighted it, and went on.

"My dear boy, the girl has not a shilling. I wished to have left you alone in peace, with your four thousand pounds: you might have lived decently upon it in Germany, where money is at 5 per cent, where your duns would not find you, and a couple of hundred a year would have kept you and your wife in comfort. But, you see, Lady Crabs would not listen to it. You had injured her; and, after she had tried to kill you and failed, she determined to ruin you, and succeeded. I must own to you that I directed the arresting business, and put her up to buying your protested bills: she got them for a trifle, and as you have paid them, has made a good two thousand pounds by her bargain. It was a painful thing to be sure, for a father to get his son arrested; but que voulez-vous! I did not appear in the transaction: she would have you ruined; and it was absolutely necessary that YOU should marry before I could, so I pleaded your cause with Miss Griffin, and made you the happy man you are. You rogue, you rogue! you thought to match your old father, did you? But, never mind; lunch will be ready soon. In the meantime, have a segar, and drink a glass of Sauterne."

Deuceace, who had been listening to this speech, sprung up wildly.

"I'll not believe it," he said: "it's a lie, an infernal lie! forged by you, you hoary villain, and by the murderess and strumpet you have married. I'll not believe it; show me the will. Matilda! Matilda!" shouted he, screaming hoarsely, and flinging open the door by which she had gone out.

"Keep your temper, my boy. You ARE vexed, and I feel for you: but don't use such bad language: it is quite needless, believe me."

"Matilda!" shouted out Deuceace again; and the poor crooked thing came trembling in, followed by Miss Kicksey.

"Is this true, woman?" says he, clutching hold of her hand.

"What, dear Algernon?" says she.

"What?" screams out Deuceace,—"what? Why that you are a beggar, for marrying without your mother's consent—that you basely lied to me, in order to bring about this match—that you are a swindler, in conspiracy with that old fiend yonder and the she-devil his wife?"

"It is true," sobbed the poor woman, "that I have nothing; but—"

"Nothing but what? Why don't you speak, you drivelling fool?"

"I have nothing!—but you, dearest, have two thousand a year. Is that not enough for us? You love me for myself, don't you, Algernon? You have told me so a thousand times—say so again, dear husband; and do not, do not be so unkind." And here she sank on her knees, and clung to him, and tried to catch his hand, and kiss it.

"How much did you say?" says my lord.

"Two thousand a year, sir; he has told us so a thousand times."

"TWO THOUSAND! Two thou—ho, ho, ho!—haw! haw! haw!" roars my lord. "That is, I vow, the best thing I ever heard in my life. My dear creature, he has not a shilling—not a single maravedi, by all the gods and goddesses." And this exlnt noblemin began laffin louder than ever: a very kind and feeling genlmn he was, as all must confess.

There was a paws: and Mrs. Deuceace didn begin cussing and swearing at her husband as he had done at her: she only said, "O Algernon! is this true?" and got up, and went to a chair and wep in quiet.

My lord opened the great box. "If you or your lawyers would like to examine Sir George's will, it is quite at your service; you will see here the proviso which I mentioned, that gives the entire fortune to Lady Griffin—Lady Crabs that is: and here, my dear boy, you see the danger of hasty conclusions. Her ladyship only showed you the FIRST PAGE OF THE WILL, of course; she wanted to try you. You thought you made a great stroke in at once proposing to Miss Griffin—do not mind it, my love, he really loves you now very sincerely!—when, in fact, you would have done much better to have read the rest of the will. You were completely bitten, my boy—humbugged, bamboozled—ay, and by your old father, you dog. I told you I would, you know, when you refused to lend me a portion of your Dawkins money. I told you I would; and I DID. I had you the very next day. Let this be a lesson to you, Percy my boy; don't try your luck again against such old hands: look deuced well before you leap: audi alteram partem, my lad, which means, read both sides of the will. I think lunch is ready; but I see you don't smoke. Shall we go in?"

"Stop, my lord," says Mr. Deuceace, very humble: "I shall not share your hospitality—but—but you know my condition; I am penniless—you know the manner in which my wife has been brought up—"

"The Honorable Mrs. Deuceace, sir, shall always find a home here, as if nothing had occurred to interrupt the friendship between her dear mother and herself."

"And for me, sir," says Deuceace, speaking faint, and very slow; "I hope—I trust—I think, my lord, you will not forget me?"

"Forget you, sir; certainly not."

"And that you will make some provision—?"

"Algernon Deuceace," says my lord, getting up from the sophy, and looking at him with sich a jolly malignity, as I never see, "I declare, before heaven, that I will not give you a penny!"

Hereupon my lord held out his hand to Mrs. Deuceace, and said, "My dear, will you join your mother and me? We shall always, as I said, have a home for you."

"My lord," said the poar thing, dropping a curtsy, "my home is with HIM!"

About three months after, when the season was beginning at Paris, and the autumn leafs was on the ground, my lord, my lady, me and Mortimer, were taking a stroal in the Boddy Balong, the carridge driving on slowly ahead, and us as happy as possbill, admiring the pleasant woods and the goldn sunset.

My lord was expayshating to my lady upon the exquizit beauty of the sean, and pouring forth a host of butifle and virtuous sentaments sootable to the hour. It was dalitefle to hear him. "Ah!" said he, "black must be the heart, my love, which does not feel the influence of a scene like this; gathering as it were, from those sunlit skies, a portion of their celestial gold, and gaining somewhat of heaven with each pure draught of this delicious air!"

Lady Crabs did not speak, but prest his arm and looked upwards. Mortimer and I, too, felt some of the infliwents of the sean, and lent on our goold sticks in silence. The carriage drew up close to us, and my lord and my lady sauntered slowly tords it.

Jest at the place was a bench, and on the bench sate a poorly drest woman, and by her, leaning against a tree, was a man whom I thought I'd sean befor. He was drest in a shabby blew coat, with white seems and copper buttons; a torn hat was on his head, and great quantaties of matted hair and whiskers disfiggared his countnints. He was not shaved, and as pale as stone.

My lord and lady didn tak the slightest notice of him, but past on to the carridge. Me and Mortimer lickwise took OUR places. As we past, the man had got a grip of the woman's shoulder, who was holding down her head sobbing bitterly.

No sooner were my lord and lady seated, than they both, with igstream dellixy and good natur, burst into a ror of lafter, peal upon peal, whooping and screaching enough to frighten the evening silents.

DEUCEACE turned round. I see his face now—the face of a devvle of hell! Fust, he lookt towards the carridge, and pinted to it with his maimed arm; then he raised the other, AND STRUCK THE WOMAN BY HIS SIDE. She fell, screaming.

Poor thing! Poor thing!

MR. YELLOWPLUSH'S AJEW

The end of Mr. Deuceace's history is going to be the end of my corrispondince. I wish the public was as sory to part with me as I am with the public; becaws I fansy reely that we've become frends, and feal for my part a becoming greaf at saying ajew.

It's imposbill for me to continyow, however, a-writin, as I have done—violetting the rules of authography, and trampling upon the fust princepills of English grammar. When I began, I knew no better: when I'd carrid on these papers a little further, and grew accustmd to writin, I began to smel out somethink quear in my style. Within the last sex weaks I have been learning to spell: and when all the world was rejoicing at the festivvaties of our youthful Quean—*when all i's were fixed upon her long sweet of ambasdors and princes, following the splendid carridge of Marshle the Duke of Damlatiar, and blinking at the pearls and dimince of Prince Oystereasy—Yellowplush was in his loanly pantry—HIS eyes were fixt upon the spelling-book—his heart was bent upon mastring the difffickleties of the littery professhn. I have been, in fact, CONVERTID.

This was written in 1838.

You shall here how. Ours, you know, is a Wig house; and ever sins his third son has got a place in the Treasury, his secknd a captingsy in the Guards, his fust, the secretary of embasy at Pekin, with a prospick of being appinted ambasdor at Loo Choo—ever sins master's sons have reseaved these attentions, and master himself has had the promis of a pearitch, he has been the most reglar, consistnt, honrabble Libbaral, in or out of the House of Commins.

Well, being a Whig, it's the fashn, as you know, to reseave littery pipple; and accordingly, at dinner, tother day, whose name do you think I had to hollar out on the fust landing-place about a wick ago? After several dukes and markises had been enounced, a very gentell fly drives up to our doar, and out steps two gentlemen. One was pail, and wor spektickles, a wig, and a white neckcloth. The other was slim with a hook nose, a pail fase, a small waist, a pare of falling shoulders, a tight coat, and a catarack of black satting tumbling out of his busm, and falling into a gilt velvet weskit. The little genlmn settled his wigg, and pulled out his ribbins; the younger one fluffed the dust of his shoes, looked at his whiskers in a little pockit-glas, settled his crevatt; and they both mounted upstairs.

"What name, sir?" says I, to the old genlmn.

"Name!—a! now, you thief o' the wurrld," says he, "do you pretind nat to know ME? Say it's the Cabinet Cyclopa—no, I mane the Litherary Chran—psha!—bluthanowns!—say it's DOCTHOR DIOCLESIAN LARNER—I think he'll know me now—ay, Nid?" But the genlmn called Nid was at the botm of the stare, and pretended to be very busy with his shoo-string. So the little genlmn went upstares alone.

"DOCTOR DIOLESIUS LARNER!" says I.

"DOCTOR ATHANASIUS LARDNER!" says Greville Fitz-Roy, our secknd footman, on the fust landing-place.

"DOCTOR IGNATIUS LOYOLA!" says the groom of the chambers, who pretends to be a scholar; and in the little genlmn went. When safely housed, the other chap came; and when I asked him his name, said, in a thick, gobbling kind of voice:

"Sawedwadgeorgeearllittnbulwig."

"Sir what?" says I, quite agast at the name.

"Sawedwad—no, I mean MISTAWedwad Lyttn Bulwig."

My neas trembled under me, my i's fild with tiers, my voice shook, as I past up the venrabble name to the other footman, and saw this fust of English writers go up to the drawing-room!

It's needless to mention the names of the rest of the compny, or to dixcribe the suckmstansies of the dinner. Suffiz to say that the two littery genlmn behaved very well, and seamed to have good appytights; igspecially the little Irishman in the whig, who et, drunk, and talked as much as a duzn. He told how he'd been presented at cort by his friend, Mr. Bulwig, and how the Quean had received 'em both, with a dignity undigscribable; and how her blessid Majisty asked what was the bony fidy sale of the Cabinit Cyclopaedy, and how be (Doctor Larner) told her that, on his honner, it was under ten thowsnd.

You may guess that the Doctor, when he made this speach, was pretty far gone. The fact is, that whether it was the coronation, or the goodness of the wine (cappitle it is in our house, I can tell you), or the natral propensaties of the gests assembled, which made them so igspecially jolly, I don't know; but they had kep up the meating pretty late, and our poar butler was quite tired with the perpechual baskits of clarrit which he'd been called upon to bring up. So that about 11 o'clock, if I were to say they were merry, I should use a mild term; if I wer to say they were intawsicated, I should use a nigspresshn more near to the truth, but less rispeckful in one of my situashn.

The cumpany reseaved this annountsmint with mute extonishment.

"Pray, Doctor Larnder," says a spiteful genlmn, willing to keep up the littery conversation, "what is the Cabinet Cyclopaedia?"

"It's the littherary wontherr of the wurrld," says he; "and sure your lordship must have seen it; the latther numbers ispicially—cheap as durrt, bound in gleezed calico, six shillings a vollum. The illusthrious neems of Walther Scott, Thomas Moore, Docther Southey, Sir James Mackintosh, Docther Donovan, and meself, are to be found in the list of conthributors. It's the Phaynix of Cyclopajies—a litherary Bacon."

"A what?" says the genlmn nex to him.

"A Bacon, shining in the darkness of our age; fild wid the pure end lambent flame of science, burning with the gorrgeous scintillations of divine litherature—a monumintum, in fact, are perinnius, bound in pink calico, six shillings a vollum."

"This wigmawole," said Mr. Bulwig (who seemed rather disgusted that his friend should take up so much of the convassation), "this wigmawole is all vewy well; but it's cuwious that you don't wemember, in chawactewising the litewawy mewits of the vawious magazines, cwonicles, weviews, and encyclopaedias, the existence of a cwitical weview and litewary chwonicle, which, though the aewa of its appeawance is dated only at a vewy few months pwevious to the pwesent pewiod, is, nevertheless, so wemarkable for its intwinsic mewits as to be wead, not in the metwopolis alone, but in the countwy—not in Fwance merely, but in the west of Euwope—whewever our pure Wenglish is spoken, it stwetches its peaceful sceptre—pewused in Amewica, fwom New York to Ningawa—wepwinted in Canada, from Montweal to Towonto—and, as I am gwatified to hear fwom my fwend the governor of Cape Coast Castle, wegularly weceived in Afwica, and twanslated into the Mandingo language by the missionawies and the bushwangers. I need not say, gentlemen—sir—that is, Mr. Speaker—I mean, Sir John—that I allude to the Litewary Chwonicle, of which I have the honor to be pwincipal contwibutor."

"Very true; my dear Mr. Bullwig," says my master: "you and I being Whigs, must of course stand by our own friends; and I will agree, without a moment's hesitation, that the Literary what-d'ye-call'em is the prince of periodicals."

"The pwince of pewiodicals?" says Bullwig; "my dear Sir John, it's the empewow of the pwess."

"Soit,—let it be the emperor of the press, as you poetically call it: but, between ourselves, confess it,—Do not the Tory writers beat your Whigs hollow? You talk about magazines. Look at—"

"Look at hwat?" shouts out Larder. "There's none, Sir Jan, compared to ourrs."

"Pardon me, I think that—"

"It is 'Bentley's Mislany' you mane?" says Ignatius, as sharp as a niddle.

"Why, no; but—"

"O thin, it's Co'burn, sure! and that divvle Thayodor—a pretty paper, sir, but light—thrashy, milk-and-wathery—not sthrong, like the Litherary Chran—good luck to it."

"Why, Doctor Lander, I was going to tell at once the name of the periodical, it's FRASER'S MAGAZINE."

"FRESER!" says the Doctor. "O thunder and turf!"

"FWASER!" says Bullwig. "O—ah—hum—haw—yes—no—why,—that is weally—no, weally, upon my weputation, I never before heard the name of the pewiodical. By the by, Sir John, what wemarkable good clawet this is; is it Lawose or Laff—?"

Laff, indeed! he cooden git beyond laff; and I'm blest if I could kip it neither,—for hearing him pretend ignurnts, and being behind the skreend, settlin somethink for the genlmn, I bust into such a raw of laffing as never was igseeded.

"Hullo!" says Bullwig, turning red. "Have I said anything impwobable, aw widiculous? for, weally, I never befaw wecollect to have heard in society such a twemendous peal of cachinnation—that which the twagic bard who fought at Mawathon has called an anewithmon gelasma."

"Why, be the holy piper," says Larder, "I think you are dthrawing a little on your imagination. Not read Fraser! Don't believe him, my lord duke; he reads every word of it, the rogue! The boys about that magazine baste him as if he was a sack of oatmale. My reason for crying out, Sir Jan, was because you mintioned Fraser at all. Bullwig has every syllable of it be heart—from the pailitix down to the 'Yellowplush Correspondence.'"

"Ha, ha!" says Bullwig, affecting to laff (you may be sure my ears prickt up when I heard the name of the "Yellowplush Correspondence"). "Ha, ha! why, to tell truth, I HAVE wead the cowespondence to which you allude: it's a gweat favowite at court. I was talking with Spwing Wice and John Wussell about it the other day."

"Well, and what do you think of it?" says Sir John, looking mity waggish—for he knew it was me who roat it.

"Why, weally and twuly, there's considewable cleverness about the cweature; but it's low, disgustingly low: it violates pwabability, and the orthogwaphy is so carefully inaccuwate, that it requires a positive study to compwehend it."

"Yes, faith," says Larner; "the arthagraphy is detestible; it's as bad for a man to write bad spillin as it is for 'em to speak wid a brrogue. Iducation furst, and ganius afterwards. Your health, my lord, and good luck to you."

"Yaw wemark," says Bullwig, "is vewy appwopwiate. You will wecollect, Sir John, in Hewodotus (as for you, Doctor, you know more about Iwish than about Gweek),—you will wecollect, without doubt, a stowy nawwated by that cwedulous though fascinating chwonicler, of a certain kind of sheep which is known only in a certain distwict of Awabia, and of which the tail is so enormous, that it either dwaggles on the gwound, or is bound up by the shepherds of the country into a small wheelbawwow, or cart, which makes the chwonicler sneewingly wemark that thus 'the sheep of Awabia have their own chawiots.' I have often thought, sir (this clawet is weally nectaweous)—I have often, I say, thought that the wace of man may be compawed to these Awabian sheep—genius is our tail, education our wheelbawwow. Without art and education to pwop it, this genius dwops on the gwound, and is polluted by the mud, or injured by the wocks upon the way: with the wheelbawwow it is stwengthened, incweased, and supported—a pwide to the owner, a blessing to mankind."

"A very appropriate simile," says Sir John; "and I am afraid that the genius of our friend Yellowplush has need of some such support."

"Apropos," said Bullwig, "who IS Yellowplush? I was given to understand that the name was only a fictitious one, and that the papers were written by the author of the 'Diary of a Physician;' if so, the man has wonderfully improved in style, and there is some hope of him."

"Bah!" says the Duke of Doublejowl; "everybody knows it's Barnard, the celebrated author of 'Sam Slick.'"

"Pardon, my dear duke," says Lord Bagwig; "it's the authoress of 'High Life,' 'Almack's,' and other fashionable novels."

"Fiddlestick's end!" says Doctor Larner; "don't be blushing and pretending to ask questions; don't we know you, Bullwig? It's you yourself, you thief of the world: we smoked you from the very beginning."

Bullwig was about indignantly to reply, when Sir John interrupted them, and said,—"I must correct you all, gentlemen; Mr. Yellowplush is no other than Mr. Yellowplush: he gave you, my dear Bullwig, your last glass of champagne at dinner, and is now an inmate of my house, and an ornament of my kitchen!"

"Gad!" says Doublejowl, "let's have him up."

"Hear, hear!" says Bagwig.

"Ah, now," says Larner, "your grace is not going to call up and talk to a footman, sure? Is it gintale?"

"To say the least of it," says Bullwig, "the pwactice is iwwegular, and indecowous; and I weally don't see how the interview can be in any way pwofitable."

But the vices of the company went against the two littery men, and everybody excep them was for having up poor me. The bell was wrung; butler came. "Send up Charles," says master; and Charles, who was standing behind the skreand, was persnly abliged to come in.

"Charles," says master, "I have been telling these gentlemen who is the author of the 'Yellowplush Correspondence' in Fraser's Magazine."

"It's the best magazine in Europe," says the duke.

"And no mistake," says my lord.

"Hwhat!" says Larner; "and where's the Litherary Chran?"

I said myself nothink, but made a bough, and blusht like pickle-cabbitch.

"Mr. Yellowplush," says his grace, "will you, in the first place, drink a glass of wine?"

I boughed agin.

"And what wine do you prefer, sir? humble port or imperial burgundy?"

"Why, your grace," says I, "I know my place, and ain't above kitchin wines. I will take a glass of port, and drink it to the health of this honrabble compny."

When I'd swigged off the bumper, which his grace himself did me the honor to pour out for me, there was a silints for a minnit; when my master said:—

"Charles Yellowplush, I have perused your memoirs in Fraser's Magazine with so much curiosity, and have so high an opinion of your talents as a writer, that I really cannot keep you as a footman any longer, or allow you to discharge duties for which you are now quite unfit. With all my admiration for your talents, Mr. Yellowplush, I still am confident that many of your friends in the servants'-hall will clean my boots a great deal better than a gentleman of your genius can ever be expected to do—it is for this purpose I employ footmen, and not that they may be writing articles in magazines. But—you need not look so red, my good fellow, and had better take another glass of port—I don't wish to throw you upon the wide world without the means of a livelihood, and have made interest for a little place which you will have under government, and which will give you an income of eighty pounds per annum; which you can double, I presume, by your literary labors."

"Sir," says I, clasping my hands, and busting into tears, "do not—for heaven's sake, do not!—think of any such think, or drive me from your suvvice, because I have been fool enough to write in magaseens. Glans but one moment at your honor's plate—every spoon is as bright as a mirror; condysend to igsamine your shoes—your honor may see reflected in them the fases of every one in the company. I blacked them shoes, I cleaned that there plate. If occasionally I've forgot the footman in the litterary man, and committed to paper my remindicences of fashnabble life, it was from a sincere desire to do good, and promote nollitch: and I appeal to your honor,—I lay my hand on my busm, and in the fase of this noble company beg you to say, When you rung your bell, who came to you fust? When you stopt out at Brooke's till morning, who sat up for you? When you was ill, who forgot the natral dignities of his station, and answered the two-pair bell? Oh, sir," says I, "I know what's what; don't send me away. I know them littery chaps, and, beleave me, I'd rather be a footman. The work's not so hard—the pay is better: the vittels incompyrably supearor. I have but to clean my things, and run my errints, and you put clothes on my back, and meat in my mouth. Sir! Mr. Bullwig! an't I right? shall I quit MY station and sink—that is to say, rise—to YOURS?"

Bullwig was violently affected; a tear stood in his glistening i. "Yellowplush," says he, seizing my hand, "you ARE right. Quit not your present occupation; black boots, clean knives, wear plush, all your life, but don't turn literary man. Look at me. I am the first novelist in Europe. I have ranged with eagle wing over the wide regions of literature, and perched on every eminence in its turn. I have gazed with eagle eyes on the sun of philosophy, and fathomed the mysterious depths of the human mind. All languages are familiar to me, all thoughts are known to me, all men understood by me. I have gathered wisdom from the honeyed lips of Plato, as we wandered in the gardens of Acadames—wisdom, too, from the mouth of Job Johnson, as we smoked our 'backy in Seven Dials. Such must be the studies, and such is the mission, in this world, of the Poet-Philosopher. But the knowledge is only emptiness; the initiation is but misery; the initiated, a man shunned and bann'd by his fellows. Oh," said Bullwig, clasping his hands, and throwing his fine i's up to the chandelier, "the curse of Pwometheus descends upon his wace. Wath and punishment pursue them from genewation to genewation! Wo to genius, the heaven-scaler, the fire-stealer! Wo and thrice bitter desolation! Earth is the wock on which Zeus, wemorseless, stwetches his withing victim—men, the vultures that feed and fatten on him. Ai, ai! it is agony eternal—gwoaning and solitawy despair! And you, Yellowplush, would penetwate these mystewies: you would waise the awful veil, and stand in the twemendous Pwesence. Beware; as you value your peace, beware! Withdwaw, wash Neophyte! For heaven's sake—O for heaven's sake!"—here he looked round with agony—"give me a glass of bwandy-and-water, for this clawet is beginning to disagwee with me."

Bullwig having concluded this spitch, very much to his own sattasfackshn, looked round to the compny for aplaws, and then swigged off the glass of brandy-and-water, giving a sollum sigh as he took the last gulph; and then Doctor Ignatius, who longed for a chans, and, in order to show his independence, began flatly contradicting his friend, addressed me, and the rest of the genlmn present, in the following manner:—

"Hark ye," says he, "my gossoon, doan't be led asthray by the nonsinse of that divil of a Bullwig. He's jillous of ye, my bhoy: that's the rale, undoubted thruth; and it's only to keep you out of litherary life that he's palavering you in this way. I'll tell you what—Plush ye blackguard,—my honorable frind the mimber there has told me a hunder times by the smallest computation, of his intense admiration of your talents, and the wonderful sthir they were making in the world. He can't bear a rival. He's mad with envy, hatred, oncharatableness. Look at him, Plush, and look at me. My father was not a juke exactly, nor aven a markis, and see, nevertheliss, to what a pitch I am come. I spare no ixpinse; I'm the iditor of a cople of pariodicals; I dthrive about in me carridge: I dine wid the lords of the land; and why—in the name of the piper that pleed before Mosus, hwy? Because I'm a litherary man. Because I know how to play me cards. Because I'm Docther Larner, in fact, and mimber of every society in and out of Europe. I might have remained all my life in Thrinity Colledge, and never made such an incom as that offered you by Sir Jan; but I came to London—to London, my boy, and now see! Look again at me friend Bullwig. He IS a gentleman, to be sure, and bad luck to 'im, say I; and what has been the result of his litherary labor? I'll tell you what; and I'll tell this gintale society, by the shade of Saint Patrick, they're going to make him a BARINET."

"A BARNET, Doctor!" says I; "you don't mean to say they're going to make him a barnet!"

"As sure as I've made meself a docthor," says Larner.

"What, a baronet, like Sir John?"

"The divle a bit else."

"And pray what for?"

"What faw?" says Bullwig. "Ask the histowy of litwatuwe what faw? Ask Colburn, ask Bentley, ask Saunders and Otley, ask the gweat Bwitish nation, what faw? The blood in my veins comes puwified thwough ten thousand years of chivalwous ancestwy; but that is neither here nor there: my political principles—the equal wights which I have advocated—the gweat cause of fweedom that I have celebwated, are known to all. But this, I confess, has nothing to do with the question. No, the question is this—on the thwone of litewature I stand unwivalled, pwe-eminent; and the Bwitish government, honowing genius in me, compliments the Bwitish nation by lifting into the bosom of the heweditawy nobility, the most gifted member of the democwacy." (The honrabble genlm here sunk down amidst repeated cheers.)

"Sir John," says I, "and my lord duke, the words of my rivrint frend Ignatius, and the remarks of the honrabble genlmn who has just sate down, have made me change the detummination which I had the honor of igspressing just now.

"I igsept the eighty pound a year; knowing that I shall ave plenty of time for pursuing my littery career, and hoping some day to set on that same bentch of barranites, which is deckarated by the presnts of my honrabble friend.

"Why shooden I? It's trew I ain't done anythink as YET to deserve such an honor; and it's very probable that I never shall. But what then?—quaw dong, as our friends say? I'd much rayther have a coat-of-arms than a coat of livry. I'd much rayther have my blud-red hand spralink in the middle of a shield, than underneath a tea-tray. A barranit I will be; and, in consiquints, must cease to be a footmin.

"As to my politticle princepills, these, I confess, ain't settled: they are, I know, necessary; but they ain't necessary UNTIL ASKT FOR; besides, I reglar read the Sattarist newspaper, and so ignirince on this pint would be inigscusable.

"But if one man can git to be a doctor, and another a barranit, and another a capting in the navy, and another a countess, and another the wife of a governor of the Cape of Good Hope, I begin to perseave that the littery trade ain't such a very bad un; igspecially if you're up to snough, and know what's o'clock. I'll learn to make myself usefle, in the fust place; then I'll larn to spell; and, I trust, by reading the novvles of the honrabble member, and the scientafick treatiseses of the reverend doctor, I may find the secrit of suxess, and git a litell for my own share. I've sevral frends in the press, having paid for many of those chaps' drink, and given them other treets; and so I think I've got all the emilents of suxess; therefore, I am detummined, as I said, to igsept your kind offer, and beg to withdraw the wuds which I made yous of when I refyoused your hoxpatable offer. I must, however—"

"I wish you'd withdraw yourself," said Sir John, bursting into a most igstrorinary rage, "and not interrupt the company with your infernal talk! Go down, and get us coffee: and, hark ye! hold your impertinent tongue, or I'll break every bone in your body. You shall have the place as I said; and while you're in my service, you shall be my servant; but you don't stay in my service after to-morrow. Go down stairs, sir; and don't stand staring here!"

In this abrupt way, my evening ended; it's with a melancholy regret that I think what came of it. I don't wear plush any more. I am an altered, a wiser, and, I trust, a better man.

I'm about a novvle (having made great progriss in spelling), in the style of my friend Bullwig; and preparing for publigation, in the Doctor's Cyclopedear, "The Lives of Eminent British and Foring Wosherwomen."

SKIMMINGS FROM "THE DAIRY OF GEORGE IV."

CHARLES YELLOWPLUSH, ESQ, TO OLIVER YORKE, ESQ.*

DEAR WHY,—Takin advantage of the Crismiss holydays, Sir John and me (who is a member of parlyment) had gone down to our place in Yorkshire for six wicks, to shoot grows and woodcox, and enjoy old English hospitalaty. This ugly Canady bisniss unluckaly put an end to our sports in the country, and brot us up to Buckly Square as fast as four posterses could gallip. When there, I found your parcel, containing the two vollumes of a new book; which, as I have been away from the literary world, and emplied solely in athlatic exorcises, have been laying neglected in my pantry, among my knife-cloaths, and dekanters, and blacking-bottles, and bed-room candles, and things.

* These Memoirs were originally published in Fraser's Magazine, and it may be stated for the benefit of the unlearned in such matters, that "Oliver Yorke" is the assumed name of the editor of that periodical.

This will, I'm sure, account for my delay in notussing the work. I see sefral of the papers and magazeens have been befoarhand with me, and have given their apinions concerning it: specially the Quotly Revew, which has most mussilessly cut to peases the author of this Dairy of the Times of George IV.*

* Diary illustrative of the Times of George the Fourth, interspersed with Original Letters from the late Queen Caroline, and from various other distinguished Persons.

"Tot ou tard, tout se scait."—MAINTENON.

In 2 vols. London, 1838. Henry Colburn.

That it's a woman who wrote it is evydent from the style of the writing, as well as from certain proofs in the book itself. Most suttnly a femail wrote this Dairy; but who this Dairy-maid may be, I, in coarse, can't conjecter: and indeed, common galliantry forbids me to ask. I can only judge of the book itself; which, it appears to me, is clearly trenching upon my ground and favrite subjicks, viz. fashnabble life, as igsibited in the houses of the nobility, gentry, and rile fammly.

But I bare no mallis—infamation is infamation, and it doesn't matter where the infamy comes from; and whether the Dairy be from that distinguished pen to which it is ornarily attributed—whether, I say, it comes from a lady of honor to the late quean, or a scullion to that diffunct majisty, no matter: all we ask is nollidge; never mind how we have it. Nollidge, as our cook says, is like trikel-possit—it's always good, though you was to drink it out of an old shoo.

Well, then, although this Dairy is likely searusly to injur my pussonal intrests, by fourstalling a deal of what I had to say in my private memoars—though many, many guineas, is taken from my pockit, by cuttin short the tail of my narratif—though much that I had to say in souperior languidge, greased with all the ellygance of my orytory, the benefick of my classcle reading, the chawms of my agreble wit, is thus abruply brot befor the world by an inferior genus, neither knowing nor writing English; yet I say, that nevertheless I must say, what I am puffickly prepaired to say, to gainsay which no man can say a word—yet I say, that I say I consider this publication welkom. Far from viewing it with enfy, I greet it with applaws; because it increases that most exlent specious of nollidge, I mean "FASHNABBLE NOLLIDGE:" compayred to witch all other nollidge is nonsince—a bag of goold to a pare of snuffers.

Could Lord Broom, on the Canady question, say moar? or say what he had tu say better? We are marters, both of us, to prinsple; and every body who knows eather knows that we would sacrafice anythink rather than that. Fashion is the goddiss I adoar. This delightful work is an offring on her srine; and as sich all her wushippers are bound to hail it. Here is not a question of trumpry lords and honrabbles, generals and barronites, but the crown itself, and the king and queen's actions; witch may be considered as the crown jewels. Here's princes, and grand-dukes and airsparent, and heaven knows what; all with blood-royal in their veins, and their names mentioned in the very fust page of the peeridge. In this book you become so intmate with the Prince of Wales, that you may follow him, if you please, to his marridge-bed: or, if you prefer the Princiss Charlotte, you may have with her an hour's tator-tator.*

Our estimable correspondent means, we presume, tete-a-tete.—O. Y.

Now, though most of the remarkable extrax from this book have been given already (the cream of the Dairy, as I wittily say,) I shall trouble you, nevertheless, with a few; partly because they can't be repeated too often, and because the toan of obsyvation with which they have been genrally received by the press, is not igsackly such as I think they merit. How, indeed, can these common magaseen and newspaper pipple know anythink of fashnabble life, let alone ryal?

Conseaving, then, that the publication of the Dairy has done reel good on this scoar, and may probly do a deal moor, I shall look through it, for the porpus of selecting the most ellygant passidges, and which I think may be peculiarly adapted to the reader's benefick.

For you see, my dear Mr. Yorke, that in the fust place, that this is no common catchpny book, like that of most authors and authoresses, who write for the base looker of gain. Heaven bless you! the Dairy-maid is above anything musnary. She is a woman of rank, and no mistake; and is as much above doin a common or vulgar action as I am superaor to taking beer after dinner with my cheese. She proves that most satisfackarily, as we see in the following passidge:—

"Her royal highness came to me, and having spoken a few phrases on different subjects, produced all the papers she wishes to have published: her whole correspondence with the prince relative to Lady J—'s dismissal; his subsequent neglect of the princess; and, finally, the acquittal of her supposed guilt, signed by the Duke of Portland, &c., at the time of the secret inquiry: when, if proof could have been brought against her, it certainly would have been done; and which acquittal, to the disgrace of all parties concerned, as well as to the justice of the nation in general, was not made public at the time. A common criminal is publicly condemned or acquitted. Her royal highness commanded me to have these letters published forthwith, saying, 'You may sell them for a great sum.' At first (for she had spoken to me before concerning this business), I thought of availing myself of the opportunity; but upon second thoughts, I turned from this idea with detestation: for, if I do wrong by obeying her wishes and endeavoring to serve her, I will do so at least from good and disinterested motives, not from any sordid views. The princess commands me, and I will obey her, whatever may be the issue; but not for fare or fee. I own I tremble, not so much for myself, as for the idea that she is not taking the best and most dignified way of having these papers published. Why make a secret of it at all? If wrong, it should not be done; if right it should be done openly, and in the face of her enemies. In her royal highness's case, as in that of wronged princes in general, why do they shrink from straightforward dealings, and rather have recourse to crooked policy? I wish, in this particular instance, I could make her royal highness feel thus: but she is naturally indignant at being falsely accused, and will not condescend to an avowed explanation."

Can anythink be more just and honrabble than this? The Dairy-lady is quite fair and abovebored. A clear stage, says she, and no favior! "I won't do behind my back what I am ashamed of before my face: not I!" No more she does; for you see that, though she was offered this manyscrip by the princess FOR NOTHINK, though she knew that she could actially get for it a large sum of money, she was above it, like an honest, noble, grateful, fashnabble woman, as she was. She aboars secrecy, and never will have recors to disguise or crookid polacy. This ought to be an ansure to them RADICLE SNEERERS, who pretend that they are the equals of fashnabble pepple; wheras it's a well-known fact, that the vulgar roagues have no notion of honor.

And after this positif declaration, which reflex honor on her ladyship (long life to her! I've often waited behind her chair!)—after this positif declaration, that, even for the porpus of DEFENDING her missis, she was so hi-minded as to refuse anythink like a peculiarly consideration, it is actually asserted in the public prints by a booxeller, that he has given her A THOUSAND POUND for the Dairy. A thousand pound! nonsince!—it's a phigment! a base lible! This woman take a thousand pound, in a matter where her dear mistriss, friend, and benyfactriss was concerned! Never! A thousand baggonits would be more prefrabble to a woman of her xqizzit feelins and fashion.

But to proseed. It's been objected to me, when I wrote some of my expearunces in fashnabble life, that my languidge was occasionally vulgar, and not such as is genrally used in those exqizzit famlies which I frequent. Now, I'll lay a wager that there is in this book, wrote as all the world knows, by a rele lady, and speakin of kings and queens as if they were as common as sand-boys—there is in this book more wulgarity than ever I displayed, more nastiness than ever I would dare TO THINK ON, and more bad grammar than ever I wrote since I was a boy at school. As for authografy, evry genlmn has his own: never mind spellin, I say, so long as the sence is right.

Let me here quot a letter from a corryspondent of this charming lady of honor; and a very nice corryspondent he is, too, without any mistake:

"Lady O—, poor Lady O—! knows the rules of prudence, I fear me, as imperfectly as she doth those of the Greek and Latin Grammars: or she hath let her brother, who is a sad swine, become master of her secrets, and then contrived to quarrel with him. You would see the outline of the melange in the newspapers; but not the report that Mr. S— is about to publish a pamphlet, as an addition to the Harleian Tracts, setting forth the amatory adventures of his sister. We shall break our necks in haste to buy it, of course crying 'Shameful' all the while; and it is said that Lady O— is to be cut, which I cannot entirely believe. Let her tell two or three old women about town that they are young and handsome, and give some well-timed parties, and she may still keep the society which she hath been used to. The times are not so hard as they once were, when a woman could not construe Magna Charta with anything like impunity. People were full as gallant many years ago. But the days are gone by wherein my lord-protector of the commonwealth of England was wont to go a lovemaking to Mrs. Fleetwood, with the Bible under his arm.

"And so Miss Jacky Gordon is really clothed with a husband at last, and Miss Laura Manners left without a mate! She and Lord Stair should marry and have children in mere revenge. As to Miss Gordon, she's a Venus well suited for such a Vulcan,—whom nothing but money and a title could have rendered tolerable, even to a kitchen wench. It is said that the matrimonial correspondence between this couple is to be published, full of sad scandalous relations, of which you may be sure scarcely a word is true. In former times, the Duchess of St. A—s made use of these elegant epistles in order to intimidate Lady Johnstone: but that ruse would not avail; so in spite, they are to be printed. What a cargo of amiable creatures! Yet will some people scarcely believe in the existence of Pandemonium.

"Tuesday Morning.—You are perfectly right respecting the hot rooms here, which we all cry out against, and all find very comfortable—much more so than the cold sands and bleak neighborhood of the sea; which looks vastly well in one of Vander Velde's pictures hung upon crimson damask, but hideous and shocking in reality. H— and his 'elle' (talking of parties) were last night at Cholmondeley House, but seem not to ripen in their love. He is certainly good-humored, and I believe, good-hearted, so deserves a good wife; but his cara seems a genuine London miss made up of many affectations. Will she form a comfortable helpmate? For me, I like not her origin, and deem many strange things to run in blood, besides madness and the Hanoverian evil.

"Thursday.—I verily do believe that I shall never get to the end of this small sheet of paper, so many unheard of interruptions have I had; and now I have been to Vauxhall, and caught the toothache. I was of Lady E. B—m and H—'s party: very dull—the Lady giving us all a supper after our promenade—

'Much ado was there, God wot
She would love, but he would not.'

He ate a great deal of ice, although he did not seem to require it: and she 'faisoit les yeux doux' enough not only to have melted all the ice which he swallowed, but his own hard heart into the bargain. The thing will not do. In the meantime, Miss Long hath become quite cruel to Wellesley Pole, and divides her favor equally between Lords Killeen and Kilworth, two as simple Irishmen as ever gave birth to a bull. I wish to Hymen that she were fairly married, for all this pother gives one a disgusting picture of human nature."

A disgusting pictur of human nature, indeed—and isn't he who moralizes about it, and she to whom he writes, a couple of pretty heads in the same piece? Which, Mr. Yorke, is the wust, the scandle or the scandle-mongers? See what it is to be a moral man of fashn. Fust, he scrapes togither all the bad stoaries about all the people of his acquentance—he goes to a ball, and laffs or snears at everybody there—he is asked to a dinner, and brings away, along with meat and wine to his heart's content, a sour stomick filled with nasty stories of all the people present there. He has such a squeamish appytite, that all the world seems to DISAGREE with him. And what has he got to say to his delicate female frend? Why that—

Fust. Mr. S. is going to publish indescent stoaries about Lady O—, his sister, which everybody's goin to by.

Nex. That Miss Gordon is going to be cloathed with an usband; and that all their matrimonial corryspondins is to be published too.

3. That Lord H. is going to be married; but there's some thing rong in his wife's blood.

4. Miss Long has cut Mr. Wellesley, and is gone after two Irish lords.

Wooden you phancy, now, that the author of such a letter, instead of writin about pipple of tip-top qualaty, was describin Vinegar Yard? Would you beleave that the lady he was a-ritin to was a chased, modist lady of honor, and mother of a family? O trumpery! O morris! as Homer says: this is a higeous pictur of manners, such as I weap to think of, as evry morl man must weap.

The above is one pritty pictur of mearly fashnabble life: what follows is about families even higher situated than the most fashnabble. Here we have the princessregient, her daughter the Princess Sharlot, her grandmamma the old quean, and her madjisty's daughters the two princesses. If this is not high life, I don't know where it is to be found; and it's pleasing to see what affeckshn and harmny rains in such an exolted spear.

"Sunday 24th.—Yesterday, the princess went to meet the Princess Charlotte at Kensington. Lady — told me that, when the latter arrived, she rushed up to her mother, and said, 'For God's sake, be civil to her,' meaning the Duchess of Leeds, who followed her. Lady — said she felt sorry for the latter; but when the Princess of Wales talked to her, she soon became so free and easy, that one could not have any FEELING about her FEELINGS. Princess Charlotte, I was told, was looking handsome, very pale, but her head more becomingly dressed,—that is to say, less dressed than usual. Her figure is of that full round shape which is now in its prime; but she disfigures herself by wearing her bodice so short, that she literally has no waist. Her feet are very pretty; and so are her hands and arms, and her ears, and the shape of her head. Her countenance is expressive, when she allows her passions to play upon it; and I never saw any face, with so little shade, express so many powerful and varied emotions. Lady — told me that the Princess Charlotte talked to her about her situation, and said, in a very quiet, but determined way, she WOULD NOT BEAR IT, and that as soon as parliament met, she intended to come to Warwick House, and remain there; that she was also determined not to consider the Duchess of Leeds as her GOVERNESS but only as her FIRST LADY. She made many observations on other persons and subjects; and appears to be very quick, very penetrating, but imperious and wilful. There is a tone of romance, too, in her character, which will only serve to mislead her.

"She told her mother that there had been a great battle at Windsor between the queen and the prince, the former refusing to give up Miss Knight from her own person to attend on Princess Charlotte as sub-governess. But the prince-regent had gone to Windsor himself, and insisted on her doing so; and the 'old Beguin' was forced to submit, but has been ill ever since: and Sir Henry Halford declared it was a complete breaking up of her constitution—to the great delight of the two princesses, who were talking about this affair. Miss Knight was the very person they wished to have; they think they can do as they like with her. It has been ordered that the Princess Charlotte should not see her mother alone for a single moment; but the latter went into her room, stuffed a pair of large shoes full of papers, and having given them to her daughter, she went home. Lady — told me everything was written down and sent to Mr. Brougham NEXT DAY."

See what discord will creap even into the best regulated famlies. Here are six of 'em—viz., the quean and her two daughters, her son, and his wife and daughter; and the manner in which they hate one another is a compleat puzzle.

The Prince hates...	{his mother
	{his wife.
	{his daughter.

Princess Charlotte hates her father.

Princess of Wales hates her husband.

The old quean, by their squobbles, is on the pint of death; and her two jewtiful daughters are delighted at the news. What a happy, fashnabble, Christian famly! O Mr. Yorke, Mr. Yorke, if this is the way in the drawin-rooms, I'm quite content to live below, in pease and charaty with all men; writin, as I am now, in my pantry, or els havin a quiet game at cards in the servants-all. With US there's no bitter, wicked, quarling of this sort. WE don't hate our children, or bully our mothers, or wish 'em ded when they're sick, as this Dairywoman says kings and queens do. When we're writing to our friends or sweethearts, WE don't fill our letters with nasty stoaries, takin away the carricter of our fellow-servants, as this maid of honor's amusin' moral frend does. But, in coarse, it's not for us to judge of our betters;—these great people are a supeerur race, and we can't comprehend their ways.

Do you recklect—it's twenty years ago now—how a bewtiffle princess died in givin buth to a poar baby, and how the whole nation of Hengland wep, as though it was one man, over that sweet woman and child, in which were sentered the hopes of every one of us, and of which each was as proud as of his own wife or infnt? Do you recklect how pore fellows spent their last shillin to buy a black crape for their hats, and clergymen cried in the pulpit, and the whole country through was no better than a great dismal funeral? Do you recklet, Mr. Yorke, who was the person that we all took on so about? We called her the Princis Sharlot of Wales; and we valyoud a single drop of her blood more than the whole heartless body of her father. Well, we looked up to her as a kind of saint or angle, and blest God (such foolish loyal English pipple as we ware in those days) who had sent this sweet lady to rule over us. But heaven bless you! it was only souperstition. She was no better than she should be, as it turns out—or at least the Dairy-maid says so. No better?—if my daughters or yours was 1/2 so bad, we'd as leaf be dead ourselves, and they hanged. But listen to this pritty charritable story, and a truce to reflexshuns:—

"Sunday, January, 9, 1814.—Yesterday, according to appointment, I went to Princess Charlotte. Found at Warwick House the harp-player, Dizzi; was asked to remain and listen to his performance, but was talked to during the whole time, which completely prevented all possibility of listening to the music. The Duchess of Leeds and her daughter were in the room, but left it soon. Next arrived Miss Knight, who remained all the time I was there. Princess Charlotte was very gracious—showed me all her bonny dyes, as B—would have called them—pictures, and cases, and jewels, &c. She talked in a very desultory way, and it would be difficult to say of what. She observed her mother was in very low spirits. I asked her how she supposed she could be otherwise? This QUESTIONING answer saves a great deal of trouble, and serves two purposes—i.e. avoids committing oneself, or giving offence by silence. There was hung in the apartment one portrait, amongst others, that very much resembled the Duke of D—. I asked Miss Knight whom it represented. She said that was not known; it had been supposed a likeness of the Pretender, when young. This answer suited my thoughts so comically I could have laughed, if one ever did at courts anything but the contrary of what one was inclined to do.

"Princess Charlotte has a very great variety of expression in her countenance—a play of features, and a force of muscle, rarely seen in connection with such soft and shadeless coloring. Her hands and arms are beautiful; but I think her figure is already gone, and will soon be precisely like her mother's: in short it is the very picture of her, and NOT IN MINIATURE. I could not help analyzing my own sensations during the time I was with her, and thought more of them than I did of her. Why was I at all flattered, at all more amused, at all more supple to this young princess, than to her who is only the same sort of person set in the shade of circumstances and of years? It is that youth, and the approach of power, and the latent views of self-interest, sway the heart and dazzle the understanding. If this is so with a heart not, I trust, corrupt, and a head not particularly formed for interested calculations, what effect must not the same causes produce on the generality of mankind?

"In the course of the conversation, the Princess Charlotte contrived to edge in a good deal of tum-de-dy, and would, if I had entered into the thing, have gone on with it, while looking at a little picture of herself, which had about thirty or forty different dresses to put over it, done on isinglass, and which allowed the general coloring of the picture to be seen through its transparency. It was, I thought, a pretty enough conceit, though rather like dressing up a doll. 'Ah!,' said Miss Knight, 'I am not content though, madame—for I yet should have liked one more dress—that of the favorite Sultana.'

"'No, no!' said the princess, 'I never was a favorite, and never can be one,'—looking at a picture which she said was her father's, but which I do not believe was done for the regent any more than for me, but represented a young man in a hussar's dress—probably a former favorite.

"The Princess Charlotte seemed much hurt at the little notice that was taken of her birthday. After keeping me for two hours and a half she dismissed me; and I am sure I could not say what she said, except that it was an olio of decousus and heterogeneous things, partaking of the characteristics of her mother, grafted on a younger scion. I dined tete-a-tete with my dear old aunt: hers is always a sweet and soothing society to me."

There's a pleasing, lady-like, moral extract for you! An innocent young thing of fifteen has pictures of TWO lovers in her room, and expex a good number more. This dellygate young creature EDGES in a good deal of TUMDEDY (I can't find it in Johnson's Dixonary), and would have GONE ON WITH THE THING (ellygence of languidge), if the dairy-lady would have let her.

Now, to tell you the truth, Mr. Yorke, I doan't beleave a single syllible of this story. This lady of honner says, in the fust place, that the princess would have talked a good deal of TUMDEDY: which means, I suppose, indeasnsy, if she, the lady of honner WOULD HAVE LET HER. This IS a good one! Why, she lets every body else talk tumdedy to their hearts' content; she lets her friends WRITE tumdedy, and, after keeping it for a quarter of a sentry, she PRINTS it. Why then, be so squeamish about HEARING a little! And, then, there's the stoary of the two portricks. This woman has the honner to be received in the frendlyest manner by a British princess; and what does the grateful loyal creature do? 2 pictures of the princess's relations are hanging in her room, and the Dairy-woman swears away the poor young princess's carrickter, by swearing they are picturs of her LOVERS. For shame, oh, for shame! you slanderin backbitin dairy-woman you! If you told all them things to your "dear old aunt," on going to dine with her, you must have had very "sweet and soothing society" indeed.

I had marked out many more extrax, which I intended to write about; but I think I have said enough about this Dairy: in fack, the butler, and the gals in the servants'-hall are not well pleased that I should go on reading this naughty book; so we'll have no more of it, only one passidge about Pollytics, witch is sertnly quite new:—

"No one was so likely to be able to defeat Bonaparte as the Crown Prince, from the intimate knowledge he possessed of his character. Bernadotte was also instigated against Bonaparte by one who not only owed him a personal hatred, but who possessed a mind equal to his, and who gave the Crown Prince both information and advice how to act. This was no less a person than Madame de Stael. It was not, as some have asserted, THAT SHE WAS IN LOVE WITH BERNADOTTE; for, at the time of their intimacy, MADAME DE STAEL WAS IN LOVE WITH ROCCA. But she used her influence (which was not small) with the Crown Prince, to make him fight against Bonaparte, and to her wisdom may be attributed much of the success which accompanied his attack upon him. Bernadotte has raised the flame of liberty, which seems fortunately to blaze all around. May it liberate Europe; and from the ashes of the laurel may olive branches spring up, and overshadow the earth!"

There's a discuvery! that the overthrow of Boneypart is owing to MADAME DE STAEL! What nonsince for Colonel Southey or Doctor Napier to write histories of the war with that Capsican hupstart and murderer, when here we have the whole affair explaned by the lady of honor!

"Sunday, April 10, 1814.—The incidents which take place every hour are miraculous. Bonaparte is deposed, but alive; subdued, but allowed to choose his place of residence. The island of Elba is the spot he has selected for his ignominious retreat. France is holding forth repentant arms to her banished sovereign. The Poissardes who dragged Louis XVI. to the scaffold are presenting flowers to the Emperor of Russia, the restorer of their legitimate king! What a stupendous field for philosophy to expatiate in! What an endless material for thought! What humiliation to the pride of mere human greatness! How are the mighty fallen! Of all that was great in Napoleon, what remains? Despoiled of his usurped power, he sinks to insignificance. There was no moral greatness in the man. The meteor dazzled, scorched, is put out,—utterly, and for ever. But the power which rests in those who have delivered the nations from bondage, is a power that is delegated to them from heaven; and the manner in which they have used it is a guarantee for its continuance. The Duke of Wellington has gained laurels unstained by any useless flow of blood. He has done more than conquer others—he has conquered himself: and in the midst of the blaze and flush of victory, surrounded by the homage of nations, he has not been betrayed into the commission of any act of cruelty or wanton offence. He was as cool and self-possessed under the blaze and dazzle of fame as a common man would be under the shade of his garden-tree, or by the hearth of his home. But the tyrant who kept Europe in awe is now a pitiable object for scorn to point the finger of derision at: and humanity shudders as it remembers the scourge with which this man's ambition was permitted to devastate every home tie, and every heartfelt joy."

And now, after this sublime passidge, as full of awfle reflections and pious sentyments as those of Mrs. Cole in the play, I shall only quot one little extrak more:—

"All goes gloomily with the poor princess. Lady Charlotte Campbell told me she regrets not seeing all these curious personages; but she says, the more the princess is forsaken, the more happy she is at having offered to attend her at this time. THIS IS VERY AMIABLE IN HER, and cannot fail to be gratifying to the princess."

So it is—wery amiable, wery kind and considerate in her, indeed. Poor Princess! how lucky you was to find a frend who loved you for your own sake, and when all the rest of the wuld turned its back kep steady to you. As for believing that Lady Sharlot had any hand in this book,* heaven forbid! she is all gratitude, pure gratitude, depend upon it. SHE would not go for to blacken her old frend and patron's carrickter, after having been so outrageously faithful to her; SHE wouldn't do it, at no price, depend upon it. How sorry she must be that others an't quite so squemish, and show up in this indesent way the follies of her kind, genrus, foolish bennyfactris!

*The "authorized" announcement, in the John Bull newspaper, sets this question at rest. It is declared that her ladyship is not the writer of the Diary.—O. Y.

CH-S Y-LL-WPL-SH, ESQ., TO SIR EDWARD LYTTON BULWER, BT. JOHN THOMAS SMITH, ESQ., TO C—S Y—H, ESQ. NOTUS.

The suckmstansies of the following harticle are as follos:—Me and my friend, the sellabrated Mr. Smith, reckonized each other in the Haymarket Theatre, during the performints of the new play. I was settn in the gallery, and sung out to him (he was in the pit), to jine us after the play, over a glass of bear and a cold hoyster, in my pantry, the family being out.

Smith came as appinted. We descorsed on the subjick of the comady; and, after sefral glases, we each of us agreed to write a letter to the other, giving our notiums of the pease. Paper was brought that momint; and Smith writing his harticle across the knife-bord, I dasht off mine on the dresser.

Our agreement was, that I (being remarkabble for my style of riting) should cretasize the languidge, whilst he should take up with the plot of the play; and the candied reader will parding me for having holtered the original address of my letter, and directed it to Sir Edward himself; and for having incopperated Smith's remarks in the midst of my own:—

MAYFAIR, Nov. 30, 1839. Midnite.

HONRABBLE BARNET!—Retired from the littery world a year or moar, I didn't think anythink would injuice me to come forrards again: for I was content with my share of reputation, and propoas'd to add nothink to those immortial wux which have rendered this Magaseen so sallybrated.

Shall I tell you the reazn of my re-appearants?—a desire for the benefick of my fellow-creatures? Fiddlestick! A mighty truth with which my busm labored, and which I must bring forth or die? Nonsince—stuff: money's the secret, my dear Barnet,—money—l'argong, gelt, spicunia. Here's quarter-day coming, and I'm blest if I can pay my landlud, unless I can ad hartificially to my inkum.

This is, however, betwigst you and me. There's no need to blacard the streets with it, or to tell the British public that Fitzroy Y-ll-wpl-sh is short of money, or that the sallybrated hauthor of the Y— Papers is in peskewniary difficklties, or is fiteagued by his superhuman littery labors, or by his famly suckmstansies, or by any other pusnal matter: my maxim, dear B, is on these pints to be as quiet as posbile. What the juice does the public care for you or me? Why must we always, in prefizzes and what not, be a-talking about ourselves and our igstrodnary merrats, woas, and injaries? It is on this subjick that I porpies, my dear Barnet, to speak to you in a frendly way; and praps you'll find my advise tolrabbly holesum.

Well, then,—if you care about the apinions, fur good or evil, of us poor suvvants, I tell you, in the most candied way, I like you, Barnet. I've had my fling at you in my day (for, entry nou, that last stoary I roat about you and Larnder was as big a bownsir as ever was)—I've had my fling at you; but I like you. One may objeck to an immense deal of your writings, which, betwigst you and me, contain more sham scentiment, sham morallaty, sham poatry, than you'd like to own; but, in spite of this, there's the STUFF in you: you've a kind and loyal heart in you, Barnet—a trifle deboshed, perhaps; a kean i, igspecially for what's comic (as for your tradgady, it's mighty flatchulent), and a ready plesnt pen. The man who says you are an As is an As himself. Don't believe him, Barnet! not that I suppose you wil,—for, if I've formed a correck apinion of you from your wucks, you think your small-beear as good as most men's: every man does,—and why not? We brew, and we love our own tap—amen; but the pint betwigst us, is this stewpid, absudd way of crying out, because the public don't like it too. Why shood they, my dear Barnet? You may vow that they are fools; or that the critix are your enemies; or that the wuld should judge your poams by your critticle rules, and not their own: you may beat your breast, and vow you are a marter, and you won't mend the matter. Take heart, man! you're not so misrabble after all: your spirits need not be so VERY cast down; you are not so VERY badly paid. I'd lay a wager that you make, with one thing or another—plays, novvles, pamphlicks, and little odd jobbs here and there—your three thowsnd a year. There's many a man, dear Bullwig that works for less, and lives content. Why shouldn't you? Three thowsnd a year is no such bad thing,—let alone the barnetcy: it must be a great comfort to have that bloody hand in your skitching.

But don't you sea, that in a wuld naturally envius, wickid, and fond of a joak, this very barnetcy, these very cumplaints,—this ceaseless groning, and moning, and wining of yours, is igsackly the thing which makes people laff and snear more? If you were ever at a great school, you must recklect who was the boy most bullid, and buffited, and purshewd—he who minded it most. He who could take a basting got but few; he who rord and wep because the knotty boys called him nicknames, was nicknamed wuss and wuss. I recklect there was at our school, in Smithfield, a chap of this milksop, spoony sort, who appeared among the romping, ragged fellers in a fine flanning dressing-gownd, that his mama had given him. That pore boy was beaten in a way that his dear ma and aunts didn't know him; his fine flanning dressing-gownd was torn all to ribbings, and he got no pease in the school ever after, but was abliged to be taken to some other saminary, where, I make no doubt, he was paid off igsactly in the same way.

Do you take the halligory, my dear Barnet? Mutayto nominy—you know what I mean. You are the boy, and your barnetcy is the dressing-gownd. You dress yourself out finer than other chaps and they all begin to sault and hustle you; it's human nature, Barnet. You show weakness, think of your dear ma, mayhap, and begin to cry: it's all over with you; the whole school is at you—upper boys and under, big and little; the dirtiest little fag in the place will pipe out blaggerd names at you, and takes his pewny tug at your tail.

The only way to avoid such consperracies is to put a pair of stowt shoalders forrards, and bust through the crowd of raggymuffins. A good bold fellow dubls his fistt, and cries, "Wha dares meddle wi' me?" When Scott got HIS barnetcy, for instans, did any one of us cry out? No, by the laws, he was our master; and wo betide the chap that said neigh to him! But there's barnets and barnets. Do you recklect that fine chapter in "Squintin Durward," about the too fellos and cups, at the siege of the bishop's castle? One of them was a brave warner, and kep HIS cup; they strangled the other chap—strangled him, and laffed at him too.

With respeck, then, to the barnetcy pint, this is my advice: brazen it out. Us littery men I take to be like a pack of schoolboys—childish, greedy, envius, holding by our friends, and always ready to fight. What must be a man's conduck among such? He must either take no notis, and pass on myjastick, or else turn round and pummle soundly—one, two, right and left, ding dong over the face and eyes; above all, never acknowledge that he is hurt. Years ago, for instans (we've no ill-blood, but only mention this by way of igsample), you began a sparring with this Magaseen. Law bless you, such a ridicklus gaym I never see: a man so belaybord, beflustered, bewolloped, was never known; it was the laff of the whole town. Your intelackshal natur, respected Barnet, is not fizzickly adapted, so to speak, for encounters of this sort. You must not indulge in combats with us course bullies of the press: you have not the STAMINY for a reglar set-to. What, then, is your plan? In the midst of the mob to pass as quiet as you can: you won't be undistubbed. Who is? Some stray kix and buffits will fall to you—mortial man is subjick to such; but if you begin to wins and cry out, and set up for a marter, wo betide you!

These remarks, pusnal as I confess them to be, are yet, I assure you, written in perfick good-natur, and have been inspired by your play of the "Sea Capting," and prefiz to it; which latter is on matters intirely pusnal, and will, therefore, I trust, igscuse this kind of ad hominam (as they say) disk-cushion. I propose, honrabble Barnit, to cumsider calmly this play and prephiz, and to speak of both with that honisty which, in the pantry or studdy, I've been always phamous for. Let us, in the first place, listen to the opening of the "Preface of the Fourth Edition:"

"No one can be more sensible than I am of the many faults and deficiencies to be found in this play; but, perhaps, when it is considered how very rarely it has happened in the history of our dramatic literature that good acting plays have been produced, except by those who have either been actors themselves, or formed their habits of literature, almost of life, behind the scenes, I might have looked for a criticism more generous, and less exacting and rigorous, than that by which the attempts of an author accustomed to another class of composition have been received by a large proportion of the periodical press.

"It is scarcely possible, indeed, that this play should not contain faults of two kinds, first, the faults of one who has necessarily much to learn in the mechanism of his art; and, secondly, of one who, having written largely in the narrative style of fiction, may not unfrequently mistake the effects of a novel for the effects of a drama. I may add to these, perhaps, the deficiencies that arise from uncertain health and broken spirits, which render the author more susceptible than he might have been some years since to that spirit of depreciation and hostility which it has been his misfortune to excite amongst the general contributors to the periodical press for the consciousness that every endeavor will be made to cavil, to distort, to misrepresent, and, in fine, if possible, to RUN DOWN, will occasionally haunt even the hours of composition, to check the inspiration, and damp the ardor.

"Having confessed thus much frankly and fairly, and with a hope that I may ultimately do better, should I continue to write for the stage (which nothing but an assurance that, with all my defects, I yet bring some little aid to the drama, at a time when any aid, however humble, ought to be welcome to the lovers of the art, could induce me to do), may I be permitted to say a few words as to some of the objections which have been made against this play?"

Now, my dear sir, look what a pretty number of please you put forrards here, why your play shouldn't be good.

First. Good plays are almost always written by actors.

Secknd. You are a novice to the style of composition.

Third. You MAY be mistaken in your effects, being a novelist by trade, and not a play-writer.

Fourthly. Your in such bad helth and sperrits.

Fifthly. Your so afraid of the critix, that they damp your arder.

For shame, for shame, man! What confeshns is these,—what painful pewling and piping! Your not a babby. I take you to be some seven or eight and thutty years old—"in the morning of youth," as the flosofer says. Don't let any such nonsince take your reazn prisoner. What, you, an old hand amongst us,—an old soljer of our sovring quean the press,—you, who have had the best pay, have held the topmost rank (ay, and DESERVED them too!—I gif you lef to quot me in sasiaty, and say, "I AM a man of genius: Y-ll-wpl-sh says so"),—you to lose heart, and cry pickavy, and begin to howl, because little boys fling stones at you! Fie, man! take courage; and, bearing the terrows of your blood-red hand, as the poet says, punish us, if we've ofended you: punish us like a man, or bear your own punishment like a man. Don't try to come off with such misrabble lodgic as that above.

What do you? You give four satisfackary reazns that the play is bad (the secknd is naught,—for your no such chicking at play-writing, this being the forth). You show that the play must be bad, and THEN begin to deal with the critix for finding folt!

Was there ever wuss generalship? The play IS bad,—your right—a wuss I never see or read. But why kneed YOU say so? If it was so VERY bad, why publish it? BECAUSE YOU WISH TO SERVE THE DRAMA! O fie! don't lay that flattering function to your sole, as Milton observes. Do you believe that this "Sea Capting" can serve the drama? Did you never intend that it should serve anything, or anybody ELSE? Of cors you did! You wrote it for money,—money from the maniger, money from the bookseller,—for the same reason that I write this. Sir, Shakspeare wrote for the very same reasons, and I never heard that he bragged about serving the drama. Away with this canting about great motifs! Let us not be too prowd, my dear Barnet, and fansy ourselves marters of the truth, marters or apostels. We are but tradesmen, working for bread, and not for righteousness' sake. Let's try and work honestly; but don't let us be prayting pompisly about our "sacred calling." The taylor who makes your coats (and very well they are made too, with the best of velvit collars)—I say Stulze, or Nugee, might cry out that THEIR motifs were but to assert the eturnle truth of tayloring, with just as much reazn; and who would believe them?

Well; after this acknollitchmint that the play is bad, come sefral pages of attack on the critix, and the folt those gentry have found with it. With these I shan't middle for the presnt. You defend all the characters 1 by 1, and conclude your remarks as follows:—

"I must be pardoned for this disquisition on my own designs. When every means is employed to misrepresent, it becomes, perhaps, allowable to explain. And if I do not think that my faults as a dramatic author are to be found in the study and delineation of character, it is precisely because THAT is the point on which all my previous pursuits in literature and actual life would be most likely to preserve me from the errors I own elsewhere, whether of misjudgment or inexperience.

"I have now only to add my thanks to the actors for the zeal and talent with which they have embodied the characters entrusted to them. The sweetness and grace with which Miss Faucit embellished the part of Violet, which, though only a sketch, is most necessary to the coloring and harmony of the play, were perhaps the more pleasing to the audience from the generosity, rare with actors, which induced her to take a part so far inferior to her powers. The applause which attends the performance of Mrs. Warner and Mr. Strickland attests their success in characters of unusual difficulty; while the singular beauty and nobleness, whether of conception or execution, with which the greatest of living actors has elevated the part of Norman (so totally different from his ordinary range of character), is a new proof of his versatility and accomplishment in all that belongs to his art. It would be scarcely gracious to conclude these remarks without expressing my acknowledgment of that generous and indulgent sense of justice which, forgetting all political differences in a literary arena, has enabled me to appeal to approving audiences—from hostile critics. And it is this which alone encourages me to hope that, sooner or later, I may add to the dramatic literature of my country something that may find, perhaps, almost as many friends in the next age as it has been the fate of the author to find enemies in this."

See, now, what a good comfrabble vanaty is! Pepple have quarld with the dramatic characters of your play. "No," says you; "if I AM remarkabble for anythink, it's for my study and delineation of character; THAT is presizely the pint to which my littery purshuits have led me." Have you read "Jil Blaw," my dear sir? Have you pirouzed that exlent tragady, the "Critic?" There's something so like this in Sir Fretful Plaguy, and the Archbishop of Granadiers, that I'm blest if I can't laff till my sides ake. Think of the critix fixing on the very pint for which you are famus!—the roags! And spose they had said the plot was absudd, or the langwitch absudder still, don't you think you would have had a word in defens of them too—you who hope to find frends for your dramatic wux in the nex age? Poo! I tell thee, Barnet, that the nex age will be wiser and better than this; and do you think that it will imply itself a reading of your trajadies? This is misantrofy, Barnet—reglar Byronism; and you ot to have a better apinian of human natur.

Your apinion about the actors I shan't here meddle with. They all acted exlently as far as my humbile judgement goes, and your write in giving them all possible prays. But let's consider the last sentence of the prefiz, my dear Barnet, and see what a pretty set of apiniuns you lay down.

1. The critix are your inymies in this age.

2. In the nex, however, you hope to find newmrous frends.

3. And it's a satisfackshn to think that, in spite of politticle diffrances, you have found frendly aujences here.

Now, my dear Barnet, for a man who begins so humbly with what my friend Father Prout calls an argamantum ad misericorjam, who ignowledges that his play is bad, that his pore dear helth is bad, and those cussid critix have played the juice with him—I say, for a man who beginns in such a humbill toan, it's rather RICH to see how you end.

My dear Barnet, DO you suppose that POLITTICLE DIFFRANCES prejudice pepple against YOU? What ARE your politix? Wig, I presume—so are mine, ontry noo. And what if they ARE Wig, or Raddiccle, or Cumsuvvative? Does any mortial man in England care a phig for your politix? Do you think yourself such a mity man in parlymint, that critix are to be angry with you, and aujences to be cumsidered magnanamous because they treat you fairly? There, now, was Sherridn, he who roat the "Rifles" and "School for Scandle" (I saw the "Rifles" after your play, and, O Barnet, if you KNEW what a relief it was!)—there, I say, was Sherridn—he WAS a politticle character, if you please—he COULD make a spitch or two—do you spose that Pitt, Purseyvall, Castlerag, old George the Third himself, wooden go to see the "Rivles"—ay, and clap hands too, and laff and ror, for all Sherry's Wiggery? Do you spose the critix wouldn't applaud too? For shame, Barnet! what ninnis, what hartless raskles, you must beleave them to be,—in the fust plase, to fancy that you are a politticle genus; in the secknd, to let your politix interfear with their notiums about littery merits!

"Put that nonsince out of your head," as Fox said to Bonypart. Wasn't it that great genus, Dennis, that wrote in Swiff and Poop's time, who fansid that the French king wooden make pease unless Dennis was delivered up to him? Upon my wud, I doan't think he carrid his diddlusion much further than a serting honrabble barnet of my aquentance.

And then for the nex age. Respected sir, this is another diddlusion; a gross misteak on your part, or my name is not Y—sh. These plays immortial? Ah, parrysampe, as the French say, this is too strong—the small-beer of the "Sea Capting," or of any suxessor of the "Sea Capting," to keep sweet for sentries and sentries! Barnet, Barnet! do you know the natur of bear? Six weeks is not past, and here your last casque is sour—the public won't even now drink it; and I lay a wager that, betwigst this day (the thuttieth November) and the end of the year, the barl will be off the stox altogether, never, never to return.

I've notted down a few frazes here and there, which you will do well do igsamin:—

NORMAN.
"The eternal Flora
Woos to her odorous haunts the western wind;
While circling round and upwards from the boughs,
Golden with fruits that lure the joyous birds,
Melody, like a happy soul released,
Hangs in the air, and from invisible plumes
Shakes sweetness down!"

NORMAN.
"And these the lips
Where, till this hour, the sad and holy kiss
Of parting linger'd, as the fragrance left
By ANGELS when they touch the earth and vanish."

NORMAN.
"Hark! she has blessed her son! I bid ye witness,
Ye listening heavens—thou circumambient air:
The ocean sighs it back—and with the murmur
Rustle the happy leaves.
All nature breathes
Aloud—aloft—to the Great Parent's ear,
The blessing of the mother on her child."

NORMAN.
"I dream of love, enduring faith, a heart
Mingled with mine—a deathless heritage,
Which I can take unsullied to the STARS,
When the Great Father calls his children home."

NORMAN.
"The blue air, breathless in the STARRY peace,
After long silence hushed as heaven, but filled
With happy thoughts as heaven with ANGELS."

NORMAN.
"Till one calm night, when over earth and wave
Heaven looked its love from all its numberless STARS."

NORMAN.
"Those eyes, the guiding STARS by which I steered."

NORMAN.

"That great mother
(The only parent I have known), whose face
Is bright with gazing ever on the STARS—
The mother-sea."

NORMAN.
"My bark shall be our home;
The STARS that light the ANGEL palaces
Of air, our lamps."

NORMAN.
"A name that glitters, like a STAR, amidst
The galaxy of England's loftiest born."

LADY ARUNDEL.
"And see him princeliest of the lion tribe,
Whose swords and coronals gleam around the throne,
The guardian STARS of the imperial isle."

The fust spissymen has been going the round of all the papers, as real, reglar poatry. Those wickid critix! they must have been laffing in their sleafs when they quoted it. Malody, suckling round and uppards from the bows, like a happy soul released, hangs in the air, and from invizable plumes shakes sweetness down. Mighty fine, truly! but let mortial man tell the meannink of the passidge. Is it MUSICKLE sweetniss that Malody shakes down from its plumes—its wings, that is, or tail—or some pekewliar scent that proceeds from happy souls released, and which they shake down from the trees when they are suckling round and uppards? IS this poatry, Barnet? Lay your hand on your busm, and speak out boldly: Is it poatry, or sheer windy humbugg, that sounds a little melojous, and won't bear the commanest test of comman sence?

In passidge number 2, the same bisniss is going on, though in a more comprehensable way: the air, the leaves, the otion, are fild with emocean at Capting Norman's happiness. Pore Nature is dragged in to partisapate in his joys, just as she has been befor. Once in a poem, this universle simfithy is very well; but once is enuff, my dear Barnet: and that once should be in some great suckmstans, surely,—such as the meeting of Adam and Eve, in "Paradice Lost," or Jewpeter and Jewno, in Hoamer, where there seems, as it were, a reasn for it. But sea-captings should not be eternly spowting and invoking gods, hevns, starrs, angels, and other silestial influences. We can all do it, Barnet; nothing in life is esier. I can compare my livry buttons to the stars, or the clouds of my backopipe to the dark vollums that ishew from Mount Hetna; or I can say that angels are looking down from them, and the tobacco silf, like a happy sole released, is circling round and upwards, and shaking sweetness down. All this is as esy as drink; but it's not poatry, Barnet, nor natural. People, when their mothers reckonize them, don't howl about the suckumambient air, and paws to think of the happy leaves a-rustling—at least, one mistrusts them if they do. Take another instans out of your own play. Capting Norman (with his eternil SLACK-JAW!) meets the gal of his art:—

"Look up, look up, my Violet—weeping? fie!
And trembling too—yet leaning on my breast.
In truth, thou art too soft for such rude shelter.
Look up! I come to woo thee to the seas,

My sailor's bride! Hast thou no voice but blushes?
Nay—From those roses let me, like the bee,
Drag forth the secret sweetness!

VIOLET.
"Oh what thoughts
Were kept for SPEECH when we once more should meet,
Now blotted from the PAGE; and all I feel
Is—THOU art with me!"

Very right, Miss Violet—the scentiment is natral, affeckshnit, pleasing, simple (it might have been in
more grammaticle languidge, and no harm done); but never mind, the feeling is pritty; and I can fancy,
my dear Barnet, a pritty, smiling, weeping lass, looking up in a man's face and saying it. But the
capting!—oh, this capting!—this windy, spouting captain, with his prittinesses, and conseated apollogies
for the hardness of his busm, and his old, stale, vapid similies, and his wishes to be a bee! Pish! Men
don't make love in this finniking way. It's the part of a sentymentle, poeticle taylor, not a galliant
gentleman, in command of one of her Madjisty's vessels of war.

Look at the remaining extrac, honored Barnet, and acknollidge that Capting Norman is eturnly repeating
himself, with his endless jabber about stars and angels. Look at the neat grammaticle twist of Lady
Arundel's spitch, too, who, in the corse of three lines, has made her son a prince, a lion, with a sword
and coronal, and a star. Why jumble and sheak up metafors in this way? Barnet, one simily is quite enuff
in the best of sentences (and I preshume I kneedn't tell you that it's as well to have it LIKE, when you are
about it). Take my advise, honrabble sir—listen to a humble footmin: it's genrally best in poatry to
understand puffickly what you mean yourself, and to ingspress your meaning clearly afterwoods—in the
simpler words the better, praps. You may, for instans, call a coronet a coronal (an "ancestral coronal," p.
74) if you like, as you might call a hat a "swart sombrero," "a glossy four-and-nine," "a silken helm, to
storm impermeable, and lightsome as the breezy gossamer;" but, in the long run, it's as well to call it a
hat. It IS a hat; and that name is quite as poetticle as another. I think it's Playto, or els Harrystottle, who
observes that what we call a rose by any other name would smell as sweet. Confess, now, dear Barnet,
don't you long to call it a Polyanthus?

I never see a play more carelessly written. In such a hurry you seem to have bean, that you have actially
in some sentences forgot to put in the sence. What is this, for instance?—

"This thrice precious one
Smiled to my eyes—drew being from my breast—
Slept in my arms;—the very tears I shed
Above my treasures were to men and angels
Alike such holy sweetness!"

In the name of all the angels that ever you invoked—Raphael, Gabriel, Uriel, Zadkiel, Azrael—what does
this "holy sweetness" mean? We're not spinxes to read such durk conandrums. If you knew my state
sins I came upon this passidg—I've neither slep nor eton; I've neglected my pantry; I've been wandring
from house to house with this riddl in my hand, and nobody can understand it. All Mr. Frazier's men are
wild, looking gloomy at one another, and asking what this may be. All the cumtributors have been spoak
to. The Doctor, who knows every languitch, has tried and giv'n up; we've sent to Docteur Pettigruel, who

reads horyglifics a deal ezier than my way of spellin'—no anser. Quick! quick with a fifth edition, honored Barnet, and set us at rest! While your about it, please, too, to igsplain the two last lines:—

"His merry bark with England's flag to crown her."

See what dellexy of igspreshn, "a flag to crown her!"

"His merry bark with England's flag to crown her,
Fame for my hopes, and woman in my cares."

Likewise the following:—

"Girl, beware,
THE LOVE THAT TRIFLES ROUND THE CHARMS IT GILDS OFT RUINS WHILE IT SHINES."

Igsplane this, men and angels! I've tried every way; backards, forards, and in all sorts of trancepositions, as thus:—

The love that ruins round the charms it shines,
Gilds while it trifles oft;

Or,

The charm that gilds around the love it ruins,
Oft trifles while it shines;

Or,

The ruins that love gilds and shines around,
Oft trifles where it charms;

Or,

Love, while it charms, shines round, and ruins oft,
The trifles that it gilds;

Or,

The love that trifles, gilds and ruins oft,
While round the charms it shines.

All which are as sensable as the fust passidge.

And with this I'll alow my friend Smith, who has been silent all this time, to say a few words. He has not written near so much as me (being an infearor genus, betwigst ourselves), but he says he never had such mortial difficklty with anything as with the dixcripshn of the plott of your pease. Here his letter:—

To CH-RL-S F-TZR-Y PL-NT-G-N-T Y-LL-WPL-SH, ESQ., &c. &c.

30th Nov. 1839.

MY DEAR AND HONORED SIR,—I have the pleasure of laying before you the following description of the plot, and a few remarks upon the style of the piece called "The Sea Captain."

Five-and-twenty years back, a certain Lord Arundel had a daughter, heiress of his estates and property; a poor cousin, Sir Maurice Beevor (being next in succession); and a page, Arthur Le Mesnil by name.

The daughter took a fancy for the page, and the young persons were married unknown to his lordship.

Three days before her confinement (thinking, no doubt, that period favorable for travelling), the young couple had agreed to run away together, and had reached a chapel near on the sea-coast, from which they were to embark, when Lord Arundel abruptly put a stop to their proceedings by causing one Gaussen, a pirate, to murder the page.

His daughter was carried back to Arundel House, and, in three days, gave birth to a son. Whether his lordship knew of this birth I cannot say; the infant, however, was never acknowledged, but carried by Sir Maurice Beevor to a priest, Onslow by name, who educated the lad and kept him for twelve years in profound ignorance of his birth. The boy went by the name of Norman.

Lady Arundel meanwhile married again, again became a widow, but had a second son, who was the acknowledged heir, and called Lord Ashdale. Old Lord Arundel died, and her ladyship became countess in her own right.

When Norman was about twelve years of age, his mother, who wished to "WAFT young Arthur to a distant land," had him sent on board ship. Who should the captain of the ship be but Gaussen, who received a smart bribe from Sir Maurice Beevor to kill the lad. Accordingly, Gaussen tied him to a plank, and pitched him overboard.

About thirteen years after these circumstances, Violet, an orphan niece of Lady Arundel's second husband, came to pass a few weeks with her ladyship. She had just come from a sea-voyage, and had been saved from a wicked Algerine by an English sea captain. This sea captain was no other than Norman, who had been picked up off his plank, and fell in love with, and was loved by, Miss Violet.

A short time after Violet's arrival at her aunt's the captain came to pay her a visit, his ship anchoring off the coast, near Lady Arundel's residence. By a singular coincidence, that rogue Gaussen's ship anchored in the harbor too. Gaussen at once knew his man, for he had "tracked" him, (after drowning him,) and he informed Sir Maurice Beevor that young Norman was alive.

Sir Maurice Beevor informed her ladyship. How should she get rid of him? In this wise. He was in love with Violet, let him marry her and be off; for Lord Ashdale was in love with his cousin too; and, of course, could not marry a young woman in her station of life. "You have a chaplain on board," says her ladyship to Captain Norman; "let him attend to-night in the ruined chapel, marry Violet, and away with you to sea." By this means she hoped to be quit of him forever.

But unfortunately the conversation had been overheard by Beevor, and reported to Ashdale. Ashdale determined to be at the chapel and carry off Violet; as for Beevor, he sent Gaussen to the chapel to kill both Ashdale and Norman; thus there would only be Lady Arundel between him and the title.

Norman, in the meanwhile, who had been walking near the chapel, had just seen his worthy old friend, the priest, most barbarously murdered there. Sir Maurice Beevor had set Gaussen upon him; his reverence was coming with the papers concerning Norman's birth, which Beevor wanted in order to extort money from the countess. Gaussen was, however, obliged to run before he got the papers; and the clergyman had time, before he died, to tell Norman the story, and give him the documents, with which Norman sped off to the castle to have an interview with his mother.

He lays his white cloak and hat on the table, and begs to be left alone with her ladyship. Lord Ashdale, who is in the room, surlily quits it; but, going out, cunningly puts on Norman's cloak. "It will be dark," says he, "down at the chapel; Violet won't know me; and, egad! I'll run off with her!"

Norman has his interview. Her ladyship acknowledges him, for she cannot help it; but will not embrace him, love him, or have anything to do with him.

Away he goes to the chapel. His chaplain was there waiting to marry him to Violet, his boat was there to carry him on board his ship, and Violet was there, too.

"Norman," says she, in the dark, "dear Norman, I knew you by your white cloak; here I am." And she and the man in a cloak go off to the inner chapel to be married.

There waits Master Gaussen; he has seized the chaplain and the boat's crew, and is just about to murder the man in the cloak, when—

NORMAN rushes in and cuts him down, much to the surprise of Miss, for she never suspected it was sly Ashdale who had come, as we have seen, disguised, and very nearly paid for his masquerading.

Ashdale is very grateful; but, when Norman persists in marrying Violet, he says—no, he shan't. He shall fight; he is a coward if he doesn't fight. Norman flings down his sword, and says he WON'T fight; and—

Lady Arundel, who has been at prayers all this time, rushing in, says, "Hold! this is your brother, Percy—your elder brother!" Here is some restiveness on Ashdale's part, but he finishes by embracing his brother.

Norman burns all the papers; vows he will never peach; reconciles himself with his mother; says he will go loser; but, having ordered his ship to "veer" round to the chapel, orders it to veer back again, for he will pass the honeymoon at Arundel Castle.

As you have been pleased to ask my opinion, it strikes me that there are one or two very good notions in this plot. But the author does not fail, as he would modestly have us believe, from ignorance of stage-business; he seems to know too much, rather than too little, about the stage; to be too anxious to cram in effects, incidents, perplexities. There is the perplexity concerning Ashdale's murder, and Norman's murder, and the priest's murder, and the page's murder, and Gaussen's murder. There is the perplexity about the papers, and that about the hat and cloak, (a silly, foolish obstacle,) which only tantalize the spectator, and retard the march of the drama's action: it is as if the author had said, "I must have a new incident in every act, I must keep tickling the spectator perpetually, and never let him off until the fall of the curtain."

The same disagreeable bustle and petty complication of intrigue you may remark in the author's drama of "Richelieu." "The Lady of Lyons" was a much simpler and better wrought plot; the incidents following each other either not too swiftly or startlingly. In "Richelieu," it always seemed to me as if one heard doors perpetually clapping and banging; one was puzzled to follow the train of conversation, in the midst of the perpetual small noises that distracted one right and left.

Nor is the list of characters of "The Sea Captain" to be despised. The outlines of all of them are good. A mother, for whom one feels a proper tragic mixture of hatred and pity; a gallant single-hearted son, whom she disdains, and who conquers her at last by his noble conduct; a dashing haughty Tybalt of a brother; a wicked poor cousin, a pretty maid, and a fierce buccaneer. These people might pass three hours very well on the stage, and interest the audience hugely; but the author fails in filling up the outlines. His language is absurdly stilted, frequently careless; the reader or spectator hears a number of loud speeches, but scarce a dozen lines that seem to belong of nature to the speakers.

Nothing can be more fulsome or loathsome to my mind than the continual sham-religious clap-traps which the author has put into the mouth of his hero; nothing more unsailor-like than his namby-pamby starlit descriptions, which my ingenious colleague has, I see, alluded to. "Thy faith my anchor, and thine eyes my haven," cries the gallant captain to his lady. See how loosely the sentence is constructed, like a thousand others in the book. The captain is to cast anchor with the girl's faith in her own eyes; either image might pass by itself, but together, like the quadrupeds of Kilkenny, they devour each other. The captain tells his lieutenant to BID HIS BARK VEER ROUND to a point in the harbor. Was ever such language? My lady gives Sir Maurice a thousand pounds to WAFT him (her son) to some distant shore. Nonsense, sheer nonsense; and what is worse, affected nonsense!

Look at the comedy of the poor cousin. "There is a great deal of game on the estate—partridges, hares, wild-geese, snipes, and plovers (SMACKING HIS LIPS)—besides a magnificent preserve of sparrows, which I can sell TO THE LITTLE BLACKGUARDS in the streets at a penny a hundred. But I am very poor—a very poor old knight!"

Is this wit or nature? It is a kind of sham wit; it reads as if it were wit, but it is not. What poor, poor stuff, about the little blackguard boys! what flimsy ecstasies and silly "smacking of lips" about the plovers. Is this the man who writes for the next age? O fie! Here is another joke:—

"Sir Maurice. Mice! zounds, how can I
Keep mice! I can't afford it! They were starved
To death an age ago. The last was found
Come Christmas three years, stretched beside a bone
In that same larder, so consumed and worn
By pious fast, 'twas awful to behold it!
I canonized its corpse in spirits of wine,
And set it in the porch—a solemn warning   To thieves and beggars!"

Is not this rare wit? "Zounds! how can I keep mice?" is well enough for a miser; not too new, or brilliant either; but this miserable dilution of a thin joke, this wretched hunting down of the poor mouse! It is humiliating to think of a man of esprit harping so long on such a mean, pitiful string. A man who aspires to immortality, too! I doubt whether it is to be gained thus; whether our author's words are not too loosely built to make "starry pointing pyramids of." Horace clipped and squared his blocks more carefully before he laid the monument which imber edax, or aquila impotens, or fuga temporum might assail in vain. Even old Ovid, when he raised his stately, shining heathen temple, had placed some columns in it, and hewn out a statue or two which deserved the immortality that he prophesied (somewhat arrogantly) for himself. But let not all be looking forward to a future, and fancying that, "incerti spatium dum finiat aevi," our books are to be immortal. Alas! the way to immortality is not so easy, nor will our "Sea Captain" be permitted such an unconscionable cruise. If all the immortalities were really to have their wish, what a work would our descendants have to study them all!

Not yet, in my humble opinion, has the honorable baronet achieved this deathless consummation. There will come a day (may it be long distant!) when the very best of his novels will be forgotten; and it is reasonable to suppose that his dramas will pass out of existence, some time or other, in the lapse of the secula seculorum. In the meantime, my dear Plush, if you ask me what the great obstacle is towards the dramatic fame and merit of our friend, I would say that it does not lie so much in hostile critics or feeble health, as in a careless habit of writing, and a peevish vanity which causes him to shut his eyes to his faults. The question of original capacity I will not moot; one may think very highly of the honorable baronet's talent, without rating it quite so high as he seems disposed to do.

And to conclude: as he has chosen to combat the critics in person, the critics are surely justified in being allowed to address him directly.

With best compliments to Mrs. Yellowplush,
I have the honor to be, dear Sir,
Your most faithful and obliged humble servant,
JOHN THOMAS SMITH.

And now, Smith having finisht his letter, I think I can't do better than clothes mine lickwise; for though I should never be tired of talking, praps the public may of hearing, and therefore it's best to shut up shopp.

What I've said, respected Barnit, I hoap you woan't take unkind. A play, you see, is public property for every one to say his say on; and I think, if you read your prefez over agin, you'll see that it ax as a direct incouridgment to us critix to come forrard and notice you. But don't fansy, I besitch you, that we are actiated by hostillaty; fust write a good play, and you'll see we'll prays it fast enuff. Waiting which, Agray, Munseer le Chevaleer, l'ashurance de ma hot cumsideratun.

Voter distangy,

Y.

William Makepeace Thackeray, was born on July 18th, 1811 in Calcutta, then British India, where his father, Richmond Thackeray was the secretary to the Board of Revenue in the British East India Company. His mother, Anne Becher also worked for the British East India Company.

His father died in 1815, and his mother sent Thackeray to England the following year while she remained in India and would, sometime later, marry her childhood sweetheart. En-route to England the ship stopped for provisions on St. Helena. The Imprisoned Napoleon was pointed out to him by a servant with the words that he "eats three sheep every day, and all the little children he can lay hands on!"

Finally, back in England the young Thackeray was sent to school, initially in Southampton and Chiswick, before being moved to Charterhouse School. Charterhouse and Thackeray did not take to each other but the time became a valuable source for his later work "Slaughterhouse". Despite his less than respectful recalling of his time with them Charterhouse placed a monument in the chapel after his death.

In his final year at Charterhouse a troubling illness delayed his departure to attend Cambridge University. Over the course of his life Thackeray would suffer from ill health, much of it brought about for his fondness for "gluttling and gorging". Excess was something he could enjoy and for a man who stood some 6' 3" it would appear to the eye that, initially at least, his large frame could absorb much of that excess.

However, Thackeray's lazy attitude to completely mastering anything he set his mind too, especially where ambition for academia was involved, meant he departed Cambridge little more than a year after joining. He had however published two short works in University periodicals. As an author, he would have quite some impact on English literature in the years to come, so it seems difficult to reconcile that he felt no urgency to pursue writing at that time.

He now spent some time travelling across Europe stopping at both Paris, to study art, and to winter in Weimar. Back in London a final attempt was made on a professional career. This time studying law at Middle Temple. It lasted no more than a few months.

Now, having reached 21, he received his father's inheritance. It was a very substantial estate of 17,000 pounds, an enormous sum of money at the time. However, although Thackeray had youth he lacked a little in energy and certainly much financial experience. He funded not one but two newspapers, and neither was to prove successful. Gambling seemed enjoyable and certainly he had money to lose, which he did on a regular basis. Further investments in two soon-to-fail Indian banks quickly ensured little of his good fortune remained.

He now had to consider taking up yet another profession. Thackeray turned to art hoping that his studies in Paris would prove of benefit. Unfortunately, they did not. His ambivalent attitude continued until on August 20th, 1836 he married the 20-year-old, Isabella Gethin Shawe. It seemed to prove a turning point in many ways.

The marriage would produce three daughters; Anne Isabella in 1837, Jane, in 1838, who tragically died in infancy and Harriet Marian in 1840.

Now, as a husband and father, Thackeray seemed at last to understand his responsibilities to nurture and provide.

His early efforts at "writing for his life" were to establish his career as a foremost author. His main employment was with Fraser's Magazine, a sharp-witted and sharp-tongued conservative publication for which he produced art criticism, short fictional sketches, and who would also serialise two of his novels.

He also found time, between 1837 and 1840 to review books for The Times and to make regular contributions to The Morning Chronicle and The Foreign Quarterly Review.

In his earliest works, which he wrote under various pseudonyms including; Charles James Yellowplush, Michael Angelo Titmarsh and George Savage Fitz-Boodle, he tended towards savagery in his attacks on high society, military prowess, the institution of marriage and hypocrisy.

Between May 1839 and February 1840 Fraser's published Catherine. Originally intended as a satire of the Newgate school of crime fiction, it ended up being more of a picaresque tale. Thackeray also began work on what would eventually become A Shabby Genteel Story.

However, Thackeray, having successfully found a career that he cared about and had the talent for, found that his personal life was about to descend into chaos. After the birth of her third child in 1840, Isabella, sank into depression. At first Thackeray, didn't think too much of it. He needed to work to earn an income to support his family and finding that Isabella was distracting both herself and him he realised he could get no work done at home and so spent more and more time away until finally, in September 1840, it dawned upon him how serious his wife's condition had become. Struck by guilt, he set out with his wife to Ireland. During the boat crossing she threw herself into the sea, but was thankfully pulled from the waters. Her mother who had little understanding of her daughter's illness was of little help and perhaps a hindrance. After four-weeks they returned to England. From November 1840 to February 1842 Isabella was in and out of professional care, as her condition waxed and waned.

Isabella eventually deteriorated into a permanent state of detachment. Thackeray desperately sought cures for her, but nothing worked, and she ended up in two different asylums in or near Paris until 1845, after which Thackeray took her back to England, where he installed her with a Mrs Bakewell at Camberwell. Despite her condition Isabella would outlive her husband by 3 decades.

After his wife's illness Thackeray became a de facto widower, never able to establish another permanent relationship.

In 1843, through his connection to the illustrator John Leech, whom he had met at Charterhouse, he began writing for the newly created magazine Punch, in which he published The Snob Papers, later collected as The Book of Snobs. Thackeray was a regular contributor to Punch until 1854.

Thackeray had earlier received some success with two travel books, The Paris Sketch Book and The Irish Sketch Book, the latter marked by hostility to Irish Catholics. The book appealed to British prejudices, and on that basis Thackeray now became Punch's Irish expert, often under the pseudonym Hibernis Hibernior. It was Thackeray's writings that were the basis for Punch's notoriously harsh, hostile and condescending depictions of the Irish during the devastating Irish Famine (1845–51).

As well as his regular columns and contributions Thackeray worked on his novels. In The Luck of Barry Lyndon, which was serialised in Fraser's in 1844, he explored the situation of an outsider trying to achieve status in high society, a theme he developed more successfully a few years later with Vanity Fair.

Thackeray achieved more recognition with his Snob Papers (serialised 1846/7, and published as a book in 1848), but the work that really established his fame was the novel Vanity Fair, which first appeared in serialised instalments beginning in January 1847.

Published as a book the novel had a slow start but eventually sales rose to 7,000 copies a month. Just as importantly, it was the book that everybody was talking about. Thackeray finally had a name that gained notice and was reviewed in journals such as the famed, and much sought after, Edinburgh Review.

The accolades and success also gave him a respite from writing everything in a manner that would help ensure income rather than literary respect. Even before Vanity Fair completed its serial run Thackeray had become a celebrity, sought after by the very lords and ladies whom he satirised. with the character of Becky Sharp, the artist's daughter who rises high by manipulating all around her.

Pendennis followed in 1849-50, but it was interrupted halfway through writing for 3 months by a severe illness. Some accounts say it was cholera. Pendennis is a semi-autobiographical bildungsroman that draws on, among other things, Thackeray's disappointments in college, his ambivalent relationship with his mother, and his insider's knowledge of the London publishing world.

This novel ran at the same time as Charles Dicken's David Copperfield, and their dual appearance brought about the first of many comparisons with Dickens. Thackeray, for his part, felt that he and Dickens were battling for supremacy, though he would never equal Dickens's popularity, except with the critics.

Interestingly the two were involved in a spat which became known as the "Garrick Club affair". Thackeray and Dickens had skirmished over the "Dignity of Literature" and had other slight disagreements but this literary quarrel caused a rift in their friendship that lasted almost until the end of Thackeray's life. The relationship was healed only in Thackeray's last months, through a surprise meeting and handshake on the steps of a London club. Thackeray had taken offense at some personal remarks in a column by Edmund Yates and demanded an apology, eventually taking the affair to the Garrick Club committee. Already upset with Thackeray for an indiscreet remark about his affair with Ellen Ternan, Dickens championed Yates, helping him to write letters both to Thackeray and, in his defense, to the club's committee. Despite the intervention of Dickens, Yates eventually lost the vote of the Club's members, but the quarrel was laid out for the public in journal articles and pamphlets. "What pains me most," Thackeray said at the time, "is that Dickens should have been his adviser, and next that I should have had to lay a heavy hand on a young man who, I take it, has been cruelly punished by the issue of the affair, and I believe is hardly aware of the nature of his own offence, and doesn't even now understand that a gentleman should resent the monstrous insult which he volunteered".

Aside from these quarrelsome, distracting literary disagreements and Isabella's on-going illness life was good for Thackeray. He was to remain as he put it "at the top of the tree," for the rest of his life. The works for which he is so well remembered; Vanity Fair and Barry Lyndon had established that but he continued to write and produce novels, stories, sketches and works profusely.

To remain at such a high level in both quality and quantity is somewhat surprising given the continuation and escalation of various illnesses which continued to haunt him.

With Isabella still unwell Thackeray did seek out other women, in particular Mrs Jane Brookfield. Despite his hopes, it always felt that he was pursuing her as she battled the problems of her own marriage and turned to Thackeray for comfort and support. A source for these relationships often came on the lecture tours of Great Britain and the United States which he now entertained. These tours gave the public a chance to see and hear their hero's and provided another valuable source of income for those invited to tour. Whilst in in New York he met the Baxter family. Sally, the eldest daughter, enchanted the novelist—as a number of vibrant, intelligent, beautiful young women had done before her—and she became the model for Ethel Newcome. He visited her on his second tour of the States when she was married to a South Carolina gentleman. His choosing of married women in the shape of both Jane and Sally was ill-advised and both relationships led nowhere but did take quite some time to disassemble and for reason to set in.

In 1852, The History of Henry Esmond was published as a 3-volume novel without first being serialised and in a special type meant to imitate the appearance of an eighteenth-century book. This was the most carefully planned of Thackeray's novels. The book was celebrated for its brilliance, and Thackeray recognized it as "the very best I can do". At the time, it caused a sensation thanks to its controversial ending, wherein the hero marries a woman who early in the novel seemed more like a "mother" to him.

The eighteenth-century held a great attraction for Thackeray and he had previously set both Barry Lyndon and Catherine there as well as the sequel to Esmond, The Virginians, which takes place in North America and includes George Washington as a character.

Thackeray had twice visited the United States on lecture tours during this period as well as given lectures in London on the English humorists of the eighteenth century, and on the first four Hanoverian monarchs. The latter were published in a book as The Four Georges.

Interestingly Thackeray also decided that Politics was something he could more than dabble in. In Oxford he stood as an independent for Parliament. He was narrowly beaten by Cardwell, a politician who was substituted for the man Thackeray thought he was going to run against, although Thackeray's advocacy of entertainment on the Sabbath would have done little to help his campaign. Even so the margin of his defeat was only 1,070 votes, to Thackeray's 1,005.

In 1860 Thackeray became editor of the newly established Cornhill Magazine, a role he never felt truly comfortable in, preferring to contribute as a columnist on the Roundabout Papers. However, the financial compensation was by all accounts quite extraordinary. The Cornhill began its history with a record circulation and a number of distinguished contributors swayed onboard by Thackeray's reputation. It was in the Cornhill that he serialised his last complete novel, The Adventures of Philip in 1861-62. (After his death, the incomplete Denis Duval would also appear there in 1864).

After two years as editor he stepped down, primarily to concentrate on writing novels again. A piece he wrote for the Cornhill at this time "Thorns in the Cushion," one of The Roundabout Papers, fondly assembles the pains he felt in rejecting manuscripts on the one hand and receiving criticism of the magazine on the other. It seemed a good time to move on.

Thackeray's health had worsened during the 1850s and he was plagued by a recurring stricture of the urethra that laid him up for days at a time. He also felt that he had lost much of his creative impetus. He worsened matters by excessively eating and drinking, and avoiding exercise, though he enjoyed horseback-riding. He has been described as "the greatest literary glutton who ever lived". Indeed, his main activity apart from writing was eating and drinking and many of his stories include elaborate scenes and themes on his fondness for them.

On December 23rd, 1863, William Makepeace Thackeray, after returning from dining out and before dressing for bed, suffered a massive stroke. He was found dead on his bed the following morning. He was only fifty-two.

His death was entirely unexpected, and shocked family, friends and indeed the entire Nation.

It is said that at his funeral service thousands of mourners turned out to witness his passing. He was buried on December 29th at Kensal Green Cemetery, London.

William Makepeace Thackeray – A Concise Bibliography

The Yellowplush Papers (1837)
Catherine (1839–40)
A Shabby Genteel Story (1840)
Second Funeral of Napoleon (1841)
The Irish Sketchbook (1843)
The Luck of Barry Lyndon (1844)
Notes of a Journey from Cornhill to Grand Cairo (1846)
Mrs. Perkins's Ball (1846), under the name M. A. Titmarsh
Stray Papers: Being Stories, Reviews, Verses, and Sketches (1821-1847)
The Book of Snobs (1848)
Vanity Fair (1848)
Pendennis (1848–1850)
Rebecca and Rowena (1850)
The Paris Sketchbook (1840)
Men's Wives (1852)
The History of Henry Esmond (1852)
The English Humorists of the Eighteenth Century (1853)
The Newcomes (1855)
The Rose and the Ring (1855)
The Virginians (1857–1859)
Lovel the Widower (1860)
Four Georges (1860-1861)
The Adventures of Philip (1862)
Roundabout Papers (1863)
Denis Duval (1864)
The English Humorists of the eighteenth century: A Series of Six Lectures (1867)
Ballads (1869)
Burlesques (1869)
The Orphan of Pimlico (1876)

Thackeray wrote a numerous number of articles for magazines and the like as well as contributing many picture sketches to articles and his own books. Many were then collected and published together. We have listed his major works only for this bibliography.

www.ingramcontent.com/pod-product-compliance
Lightning Source LLC
Chambersburg PA
CBHW071410170626
46811CB00003B/1345